MED...

Chitra Datta has been a National Science Talent Search Scholar and secured the top position in MSc from IIT, Kharagpur. Her academic career culminated in a PhD in Chemistry from the University of Calcutta. She is now a manager in a multinational pharmaceutical company. She has contributed articles to *Science Reporter* and has participated in radio discussions on scientific subjects from Calcutta and Bombay A.I.R.

MEDICAL QUIZ

CHITRA DATTA

RUPA

Published by
Rupa Publications India Pvt. Ltd 2004
7/16, Ansari Road, Daryaganj
New Delhi 110002

Sales centres:

Allahabad Bengaluru Chennai
Hyderabad Jaipur Kathmandu
Kolkata Mumbai

ISBN: 978-81-716-7056-7

10 9 8 7 6 5 4

The moral right of the author has been asserted.

Printed at Gopsons Papers Ltd, Noida

To

The memory of my father
Shri Benoy Bhushan Das Gupta —
the inspiration in my life

PREFACE

Health has become a very important concept in the modern era. Under modern living conditions the hazards to good health are many, from polluted air to polluted food. This book has been designed to test the general awareness and learning urge of all who are health-conscious. Most people find it difficult, and also lack the time, to sit and decipher the technical jargon written in medical volumes and other textbooks. This book, therefore, will cater to the needs of those who would like to be aware of common ailments and diseases, their prevention, their diagnosis and cure, without scouting through volumes of text books. It will also provide common knowledge about the functioning of the human body. The book should be of interest to doctors, medical students, college students who have health and health care products in their curriculum and others who are linked with the medical profession.

This book has been presented as a quiz book, so that the reader learns while testing himself. It has been designed to cover questions from a wide range of topics that affect human health.

Drug resistance is posing a new threat to human life nowadays. Most people take medicines without any knowledge about them. Self-medication is often resorted to without any knowledge of the possible dangers. Overdose, as well as inadequate dose, of medicines is harmful to the human body. Often medication is discontinued without the knowledge of the doctor as soon as the symptoms of the disease subside. That is why drug awareness is very important these days. This book will test the reader's awareness about the different aspects of human health, and help him understand and follow the advice of medical practitioners better. However, this book does not in any way provide information for self-medication. It is very dangerous to resort to self-medication. Drugs are dangerous when they are misused or abused.

I take this opportunity to thank all my well-wishers. Special thanks are also due to my husband, S.K. Datta, for his co-operation.

Bombay
January 1991

Chitra Datta

CAUTION

The readers are warned that the information in this book should not be used for self-medication and self-treatment. The information in the book is only to test the general awareness of healthcare people and does not in any way substitute expert advice of doctors, nor does it publicize or promote any medicament. In the case of ailments the doctor should always be consulted for diagnosis and treatment, and his/her instructions followed.

CONTENTS

1

THE HUMAN BODY

Parts

1. What is the length of the colon?
   (a) Two feet (b) One and a half feet (c) Between four and six feet (d) Three feet

2. Which of the following refers to the blood vessels that surround the heart?
   (a) Fontanelles (b) Coronary vascular system (c) Profunda brachii (d) Jugular vein

3. What is the middle layer of the heart wall known as?
   (a) Myocardium (b) Pericardium (c) Atrium (d) Pyrexia

4. Erythrocytes, leucocytes and thrombocytes are present in:
   (a) Skin (b) Blood (c) Hair (d) Nails

5. Which two organs in the body are separated by the heart?
   (a) Lungs (b) Diaphragm (c) Thyroid (d) Thorax

6. Which part of the body is surrounded by membranes called meninges?
   (a) Stomach (b) Kidney (c) Brain (d) Gall bladder

7. Which part of the body is responsible for storing glycogen?
   (a) Kidney (b) Lungs (c) Trachea (d) Liver

8. What are the red blood corpuscles of blood known as?
   (a) Erythrocytes (b) Leucocytes (c) Eosinophils (d) Thrombocytes

9. What are the white blood corpuscles of blood known as?
   (a) Thrombocytes (b) Leucocytes (c) Erythroblasts (d) Erythrocytes

10. What is the other name for the thrombocytes present in blood?

(a) Platelets (b) Basophils (c) Leukoblasts
(d) Nutrophils

11. Which of the following parts of the body connects the jejunum to the stomach?

(a) Liver (b) Duodenum (c) Pancreas (d) Kidney

12. How many pairs of bones are present in the thoracic cage?

(a) Eleven (b) Ten (c) Twenty (d) Twelve

13. Which one of the following refers to the salivary gland?

(a) Thyroid gland (b) Parotid gland (c) Pineal gland (d) Bowman's gland

14. Corticotrophin, luteotrophin, thyrotrophin, follicle stimulating hormone, prolactin, and growth hormones form a group of hormones. What are these hormones known as?

(a) Pituitary hormones (b) Thyroid hormones (c) Lacrimal fluid (d) Testosterone

15. An important gland of the human body has its two lobes situated on either side of the windpipe and its location is in the neck. Which is this gland?

(a) Thyroid (b) Thymus (c) Pituitary (d) Ciliary

16. Behind the thyroid gland are situated four small glands. What are they?

(a) Haemal (b) Parathyroid (c) Ureters
(d) Parotid

17. A tiny gland with two lobes, whose size can be compared to a pea's, is situated at the bottom of the skull. Which gland is this?

(a) Adrenal (b) Pituitary (c) Islets of Langerhans (d) Parathyroid

18. Insulin is a hormone which controls the utilization of sugar in the body. Lack of insulin causes diabetes mellitus. Which gland in the body is responsible for secreting insulin?

(a) Pineal (b) Thymus (c) Pituitary (d) Pancreas

19. Which gland is responsible for secreting the female sex hormones oestrogen and progesterone?

13

(a) Skene's glands (b) Ovaries (c) Adrenal
(d) Thyroid

20. The bile secreted by the liver is stored in a pear-shaped bag. From this bag the bile is transported to the duodenum. Which is this bag?
(a) Pancreas (b) Gall bladder (c) Kidney
(d) Ureters

21. At the back of the belly, on either side of the spine, there exist a couple of bean-shaped organs. What are they?
(a) Appendix (b) Ovaries (c) Cervix (d) Kidneys

22. An organ which does not help the body in any way is located at the place where the large and small intestines join each other. What is this known as?
(a) Appendix (b) Jejunum (c) Ileum (d) Globus

23. Hereditary characteristics which determine the blood group, colour of skin, hair, mental ability, etc., are controlled by certain particles present inside the cells. What are they?
(a) Enzymes (b) Genes (c) Red blood cells
(d) Phagocytes

24. The cells of the body contain small bodies which carry the genes that are responsible for hereditary characteristics. What are these known as?
(a) Chorea (b) Platelets (c) Chromosomes
(d) White blood cells

25. Twenty-two pairs of ordinary chromosomes and a pair of X-chromosomes are present in the cells of:
(a) A man (b) A woman (c) A cat (d) Hermaphrodites

26. Twenty-two pairs of ordinary chromosomes, one X-chromosome and one Y-chromosome are present in the cells of:
(a) A woman (b) A man (c) All mammals (d) Fish

27. The nose, pharynx, larynx, trachea, bronchi, bronchioles and lungs make up:

(a) The respiratory system (b) The digestive system (c) The reproductive system (d) The nervous system

28. The abdomen is separated from the chest by a muscle. Which is this?
(a) Liver (b) Diaphragm (c) Lungs (d) Heart

29. The enzymes amylase, lipase, and trypsin are present in:
(a) Pancreatic juice (b) Gastric juice (c) Bile (d) Blood

30. What are the nerve cells present in the brain known as?
(a) Glia (b) Neurons (c) RNA (d) DNA

31. What is the top layer of the skin known as?
(a) Follicles (b) Epidermis (c) Pores (d) Corium

32. What is the bottom layer of the skin known as?
(a) Succulus (b) Polypus (c) Dermis (d) Nystagmus

33. In which part of the skin are sweat glands, oil glands, pores, nerves, and blood vessels situated?
(a) Dermis (b) Stratum corneum (c) Stratum lucidum (d) Stratum granulosum

34. What are sebaceous glands?
(a) Sweat glands (b) Oil glands (c) Thyroid gland (d) Pituitary gland

35. In which part of the body is the Adam's apple located?
(a) Hands (b) Stomach (c) Legs (d) Throat

36. How many bones are there in the spinal column?
(a) 33 (b) 36 (c) 73 (d) 45

37. Which of the following is a part of the nail?
(a) Myringa (b) Lunula (c) Fat (d) Finger

38. Which of the following is a leg bone?
(a) Tibia (b) Scapula (c) Ulna (d) Ileum

39. The islets of Langerhans are cells that manufacture insulin in the body. Where in the body can these cells be located?
(a) Liver (b) Kidney (c) Stomach (d) Pancreas

40. Which of the following are present at the back of the upper eyelids?
(a) Parotid gland (b) Nits (c) Lacrimal gland (d) Endocrine glands
41. Which of the following refers to the collar bone?
(a) Maxilla (b) Clavicle (c) Sternum (d) Humerus

Functions
42. In which part of the body does absorption of water and nutrients into the blood from the bowel content takes place?
(a) Colon (b) Kidney (c) Stomach (d) Liver
43. Ultraviolet rays falling on the skin convert 7-dehydrocholesterol into:
(a) Vitamin D (b) Vitamin B_1 (c) Biotin (d) Niacin
44. Which of the following chemical agents is a neurotransmitter?
(a) Thrombodyn (b) Citric acid (c) Ascorbic acid (d) Norepinephrine
45. The organ in the body which helps in the metabolism of fats and proteins is also responsible for the secretion of bile. Which one is it?
(a) Pancreas (b) Duodenum (c) Liver (d) Kidney
46. The delicate nerve tissues of the brain are protected from shocks by:
(a) Fat deposits inside the brain (b) A fluid inside the brain (c) Proteins inside the brain (d) Calcium deposits inside the brain
47. Which part of the body is responsible for the oxygenation of blood?
(a) Brain (b) Heart (c) Lungs (d) Appendix
48. Cavities in bones are filled with marrow. What is the function of the marrow?
(a) To produce lipids (b) To produce vitamins (c) To produce blood (d) To produce proteins
49. An enzyme which is secreted by the salivary glands is responsible for converting starch into sugar. Which enzyme is it?

(a) Ptyalin (b) Pepsin (c) Trypsin (d) Polypeptides
50. Which enzyme is responsible for converting the sugar present in milk into glucose?
(a) Pepsin (b) Lactase (c) Amylase (d) Protease
51. Which of the following enzymes is responsible for the breaking down of proteins?
(a) Papain (b) β-Lactamase (c) Pepsin (d) Both a and b
52. Two important hormones are secreted by the thyroid gland. These hormones govern the speed at which energy is used by the body. Which are these hormones?
(a) Oestrogen, Progesterone (b) Aldosterone, Testosterone (c) Thyroxine, Triiodothyronine, (d) Cortisone, Hydrocortisone
53. Which gland is responsible for secreting the juice containing the enzymes trypsin and amylopsin?
(a) Thymus (b) Pancreas (c) Pituitary (d) Ovaries
54. Certain hormones govern the growth taking place in the body. Which are they?
(a) Sex hormones (b) Pancreatic hormones (c) Pituitary hormones (d) Renal hormones
55. It is essential for the blood circulating in the body to be kept pure. Waste products like urea and surplus water are filtered out of the blood and excreted as urine. Which organ does this function of filtering?
(a) Ureter (b) Kidney (c) Colon (d) Urethra
56. The pituitary glands, the temperature of the body, and the emotions of an individual are controlled by a portion of the brain known as:
(a) Hypothalamus (b) Duramater (c) Piamater (d) Medulla oblongata
57. Which part of the heart pumps blood through the whole body?
(a) Left auricles (b) Left ventricle (c) Pericardium (d) Aorta

58. Which part of the heart is responsible for circulating blood through the lungs?
(a) Right atria (b) Myocardium (c) Veins (d) Right ventricle
59. From which part of the body are digested foods absorbed and passed into the blood stream?
(a) Large intestine (b) Liver (c) Small intestine (d) Stomach
60. There are certain cells in the body whose function is to form bones. What are these cells known as?
(a) B-cells (b) T-cells (c) Islets of Langerhans (d) Osteoblasts
61. Where are proteins digested?
(a) Ascending colon (b) Pancreas (c) Descending colon (d) Stomach and small intestine
62. Which of the following aids in controlling body temperature?
(a) Stomach (b) Liver (c) Skin (d) Hair
63. What is the function of the lacrimal glands?
(a) To secrete tears (b) To secrete oil (c) To secrete hormones (d) To secrete enzymes

Miscellaneous
64. One often hears the word pulmonary being used. What does it refer to?
(a) Heart (b) Stomach (c) Lungs (d) Pancreas
65. What does the word cardiac refer to?
(a) Heart (b) Brain (c) Lungs (d) Liver
66. Which one of the following refers to the normal body temperature?
(a) Normothermia (b) Hyperthermia (c) Hypothermia (d) Thermalgia
67. What is the approximate weight of the liver?
(a) 3.5 to 5.5 kg (b) 4.5 to 5.3 kg (c) 1.5 to 1.8 kg (d) 7 to 8 kg
68. Which is the largest organ in the body?
(a) Heart (b) Kidney (c) Liver (d) Stomach

69. Which one of the following can be used to describe plasma?
   (a) Fluid present in liver (b) Fluid present in blood (c) Fluid present in lungs (d) Fluid present in kidney

70. Which one of the following is found in bones?
   (a) Calcium phosphate (b) Sodium phosphate (c) Potassium chloride (d) Sodium carbonate

71. It has been found that the red coloured bone marrow changes into a yellow colour with age. What may be the reason for this?
   (a) Deposition of salt (b) Deposition of fat (c) Deposition of protein (d) Deposition of sugar

72. Secretions of the endocrine glands like the thyroid glands and pituitary glands are known as:
   (a) Hormones (b) Chromocrinia (c) Cerumen (d) Sebum

73. The function of the bile is to digest fats. What is the other name for bile?
   (a) Bilirubin (b) Gall (c) Biliverdin (d) Glia

74. The secretion of the sebaceous glands is oily in nature. What is it known as?
   (a) Sweat (b) Mucus (c) Sebum (d) Pus

75. Which enzyme is present in tears?
   (a) Lactase (b) Amylase (c) Lacrimase (d) Lipase

2
COMMON AILMENTS AND DISEASES

General Information

76. Bacteria that produce diseases are known as:
   (a) Aerogenes (b) Nonpathogenic bacteria (c) Saprophytes (d) Pathogenic bacteria

77. Rabies is a disease produced by a virus. In which category does the rabies virus belong?
   (a) Rhabdovirus (b) Picornavirus (c) Mosaic virus (d) Myxovirus

78. Insects and ticks are known to be carriers of some viruses. What are these viruses known as?
(a) Poxviruses (b) Herpesviruses (c) Arenaviruses (d) Arboviruses

79. It has been found that viruses have either RNA or DNA but not both. Which of the following belong to the category of RNA virus?
(a) Adenoviruses (b) Reoviruses (c) Togavirus (d) Papovaviruses

80. In which of the following groups do the poxviruses and herpesviruses belong?
(a) RNA viruses (b) DNA viruses (c) Street virus (d) Mosaic virus

81. When the body is under foreign invasion it manufactures certain proteins to fight against the foreign proteins. What are these known as?
(a) Allergen (b) Myosin (c) Antibodies (d) Albumin

82. What is the science of medicine known as?
(a) Skeletology (b) Sitology (c) Otology (d) Iatrology

83. What conditions are ideal for the growth of bacteria?
(a) Moisture, food, warm and dark conditions (b) Cold, moisture, and light (c) Severe cold, dry and dark conditions (d) Very hot and dry conditions

AIDS

84. What is AIDS?
(a) Acquired Immuno-Deficiency Syndrome (b) An Immuno-Deficiency Syndrome (c) Anti Immuno-Deficiency Syndrome (d) Auto Immune Diseases

85. Which part of the human system does AIDS attack?
(a) Heart (b) Stomach (c) Liver (d) Immune system

86. What is the name of the virus responsible for AIDS?

(a) Cytomegalovirus (b) Varicella-zoster virus (c) Human Immunodeficiency virus (d) Acquired Immuno-Deficiency Syndrome virus

87. An antibody is present in most AIDS patients. Which one is it?

(a) Antitoxins (b) Glycoprotein-41 (c) Agglutinins (d) Bacteriolysins

88. How is AIDS transmitted?

(a) Blood and body fluids (b) Water (c) Food (d) Air

89. To which one of the following types does the virus which causes AIDS belong?

(a) Poxvirus (b) DNA virus (c) RNA virus (d) Herpesvirus

90. What is the length of the incubation period of the virus responsible for AIDS?

(a) One year (b) One month (c) Six months (d) Many years

91. Which of the following cells does the Human Immunodeficiency Virus attack?

(a) B cells (b) T-helper cells (c) T-memory cells (d) Myeloma cells

92. The level of which antibody goes down as the AIDS disease progresses in a patient?

(a) p24 (b) IgM_1 (c) IgG_4 (d) IgA_1

93. What is the other name for antibodies?

(a) Immunoglobulins (b) Antigen (c) Allergen (d) Isoantibody

94. When was the Human Immunodeficiency Virus identified as the causative factor of AIDS?

(a) 1986 (b) 1987 (c) 1983 (d) 1989

Giardiasis

95. Which parasite is responsible for giardiasis?

(a) E-histolytica (b) Giardia lamblia (c) Myxovirus (d) Rhabdovirus

96. Where is the parasite responsible for giardiasis prevalent?
    (a) Areas where sanitation is poor (b) Dry areas (c) Congested areas (d) Thinly populated areas
97. What are the effects of acute giardiasis?
    (a) Kidney damage (b) Liver damage (c) The function of the intestine is hindered and growth is obstructed (d) Damage to the stomach
98. What happens to the excreted cysts of Giardia lamblia?
    (a) Die as soon as they are excreted (b) Remain alive even after excretion (c) Rarely multiply (d) Remain alive for a few seconds

Amoebiasis
99. Which parasite is responsible for amoebiasis?
    (a) Entamoeba histolytica (b) Arenavirus (c) Togavirus (d) Bacillus saprogenes
100. How does the parasite responsible for amoebiasis enter the human system?
    (a) Through respiration (b) Through touch (c) Through faecal contamination (d) Through blood transfusion
101. Where in the human body do these parasites lodge themselves?
    (a) Pancreas (b) Duodenum (c) Coion (d) Stomach
102. What happens when these parasites invade the intestinal wall?
    (a) Amoebic dysentery (b) Colitis (c) Gastritis (d) Piles

Diseases of the eye
103. When distant objects cannot be seen by a person clearly, he is said to be suffering from:
    (a) Myopia (b) Glaucoma (c) Hypermetropia (d) Diplopia

104. When nearby objects cannot be seen by a person, he is said to be suffering from:
(a) Cataract (b) Longsightedness (c) Myopia (d) Anopia

105. In which of the following are images not focused on the retina properly?
(a) Xanthoma (b) Oncocerciasis (c) Astigmatism (d) Xerophthalmia

106. When the lens of the eyes become cloudy and opaque, what is the condition known as?
(a) Cataract (b) Iritis (c) Anatropia (d) Ablepsia

107. Cataract formed as a result of a person's old age is known as:
(a) Old cataract (b) Senile cataract (c) Old age cataract (d) Mature cataract

108. Cataracts can also happen as a result of:
(a) Iritis (b) Squint (c) Anaphoria (d) Catatropia

109. In which of the following does the building up of pressure inside the eyes lead to blindness?
(a) Myopia (b) Astigmatism (c) Hypermetropia (d) Glaucoma

110. When inflammation occurs of the membrane lining the inner surface of the eyelids, it is known as:
(a) Micropsia (b) Phacocele (c) Conjunctivitis (d) Retinoblastoma

111. When the muscles of the eyes are not balanced, resulting in non-alignment of the eyes, it gives rise to a condition known as:
(a) Squint (b) Blindness (c) Xerophthalmia (d) Xanthoma

112. In which of the following conditions does the vision decrease?
(a) Ptosis (b) Amblyopia (c) Photophobia (d) None

113. In which of the following do malignant tumours grow in the eyes?
(a) Sarcoma (b) Lymphoma (c) Retinoblastoma (d) Buhl's disease

114. Which of the following is an eye disorder arising from a genetic disorder?
(a) Iritis (b) Cataract (c) Uveitis (d) Red-green colour blindness

Leprosy
115. In which of the following parts of the world is leprosy prevalent?
(a) Japan (b) Asia (c) USA (d) USSR
116. Which organism is responsible for producing leprosy?
(a) Mycobacterium leprae (b) B. aerogenes (c) B-alcaligines (d) Corynebacterium diphtheriae
117. What is Mycobacterium leprae?
(a) A virus (b) A bacterium (c) A tick (d) Fungus
118. How does Mycobacterium leprae enter the body?
(a) Through food (b) Through water (c) Through respiration and skin (d) Through blood transfusion
119. How is leprosy transmitted?
(a) From person to person (b) Through air (c) Through infected needles (d) Through contaminated water

Cancer
120. When the tissues in the body grow in an abnormal manner, it gives rise to:
(a) Stye (b) Tumour (c) Inflammation (d) Hypertrophy
121. Tumours are often referred to as:
(a) Moles (b) Cysts (c) Neoplasms (d) Malignant boils
122. When cancer attacks the bone marrow, it is known as:
(a) Leukaemia (b) Adenoma (c) Fibroma (d) Myoma
123. A non-malignant tumour made up of fat tissues is known as:

24

(a) Sarcoma (b) Carcinoma (c) Melanoma (d) Lipoma
124. What is cancer of the lymphoid tissues known as?
(a) Neuroma (b) Glioma (c) Lymphoma (d) Ecchymoma
125. Cancer of the mucous membranes, skin, secretory glands, etc., is known as:
(a) Carcinoma (b) Glenard's disease (c) Fibroid (d) Osteoma
126. Cancer of the bones, muscles, kidneys, pigmented tissues, lungs, cartilages, etc., is known as:
(a) Haematoma (b) Hyposalemia (c) Adenoma (d) Sarcoma
127. What is chondrosarcoma?
(a) Cancer of the cartilage (b) Blood cancer (c) Lung cancer (d) Brain tumour
128. What is osteosarcoma?
(a) Blood cancer (b) Cervical cancer (c) Cancer of the bone (d) Breast cancer
129. What is melanotic sarcoma?
(a) Brain tumour (b) Lung cancer (c) Cancer of the pigmented tissue (d) Ovarian tumour
130. What is myosarcoma?
(a) Cancer of the muscles (b) Skin cancer (c) Oral cancer (d) Cancer of the sebaceous gland
131. A tumour that occurs in the nerve tissues of the brain is known as:
(a) Chondroma (b) Glioma (c) Papilloma (d) Myxoma
132. Cells that divide abnormally at a much faster rate than normal cells are known as:
(a) Epithelial cells (b) Endothelium cells (c) Cancerous cells (d) Osteoblasts
133. What are carcinogens?
(a) Agents that cause cancer (b) Agents that cause fever (c) Agents that cause dyspnoea (d) Agents that cause hypertension
134. What happens in Hodgkin's disease?

(a) The pancreas are enlarged (b) The ovaries are enlarged (c) The heart is enlarged (d) The lymphatic glands are enlarged

135. Heavy smokers and drinkers are prone to:
(a) Oesophageal cancer (b) Stomach cancer (c) Skin cancer (d) Cancer of the muscles

136. A tumour that grows slowly and confines itself to a certain part of the body and does not spread rapidly is known as:
(a) Sarcoma (b) Carcinoma (c) Benign tumour (d) Melanoma

137. When tumours interfere with the functions of the body and grow and spread swiftly, they are known as:
(a) Malignant tumours (b) Warts (c) Heterologous tumour (d) Dentinoid tumours

138. A tumour of the abdomen in children which mostly affects the kidneys is known as:
(a) Wilm's tumour (b) Myoma (c) Chondroma (d) Fibroma

139. When malignancy appears in the cells of the liver, it is known as:
(a) Hodgkin's disease (b) Hepatic fibrosis (c) Malignant hepatoma (d) Liver abscess

140. What is the disease known as in which cancer strikes the cells that manufacture insulin in the body?
(a) Insuloma (b) Black cancer (c) Pancreatitis (d) Mollis cancer

141. When a tumour grows in the sweat glands, what is the disease known as?
(a) Chemosis (b) Melanoma (c) Miliaria (d) Syringadenoma

142. In which of the following diseases do the tongue, lips, and cheeks get affected?
(a) Kaposi's sarcoma (b) Lung cancer (c) Lipoma (d) Glioma

143. What is a neoplasm of the spleen known as?

(a) Angioma (b) Splenoma (c) Abscess of spleen
(d) Aran's green cancer

Tuberculosis

144. Which bacillus is responsible for causing tuberculosis?
(a) Mycobacterium tuberculosis (b) Mycobacterium leprae (c) B.acidophilus (d) Bacillus subtilis

145. When tuberculosis affects the spine, what is the disease known as?
(a) Ptosis (b) Pott's disease (c) Kyphosis
(d) Bright's disease

146. Which of the following refers to tuberculosis of the lungs?
(a) Pulmonitis (b) Pulmonary tuberculosis
(c) Pneumoculosis (d) Laryngeal tuberculosis

147. Tuberculosis affects the bones also. What is this form of tuberculosis known as?
(a) Tuberculous osteomyelitis (b) Miliary tuberculosis (c) Pleural tuberculosis (d) Hypocalcaemia

148. When tuberculosis attacks the lymph glands, it is known as:
(a) Attenuated tuberculosis (b) Pulmonary tuberculosis (c) Tuberculosis adenitis (d) Avian tuberculosis

149. Tuberculosis is also known to affect the joints. What is this form of tuberculosis known as?
(a) Filariasis (b) Tuberculous arthritis (c) Pott's disease (d) Rheumatoid arthritis

Cerebral haemorrhage

150. Which of the following can attack patients suffering from high blood pressure, hardening of the arteries, and swelling of the walls of the arteries?
(a) Frequent fever (b) Cerebral haemorrhage
(c) Kidney damage (d) Liver damage

151. When the arteries become hard and stiff in a person, the person is said to be suffering from:
(a) Arteriosclerosis (b) Aneurysm (c) Arteriorhexis (d) Arteriosteosis

152. In which part of the body does the blood vessel rupture in cerebral haemorrhage?
(a) Heart (b) Lungs (c) Brain (d) Stomach

153. An attack of cerebral haemorrhage leads to:
(a) Excitement (b) Unconsciousness and paralysis (c) Convulsions (d) Fits

Ulcers

154. What is an open sore known as?
(a) Cancer (b) Ulcer (c) Dermatitis (d) Myelin

155. When ulceration of the digestive system occurs, it is known as:
(a) Peptic ulcer (b) Colitis (c) Hay fever (d) Appendicitis

156. When ulceration takes place in the upper part of the small intestine, it is known as:
(a) Gastric ulcer (b) Granulitis (c) Duodenal ulcer (d) Haemorrhage

157. Ulceration of the stomach is known as:
(a) Gastric ulcer (b) Diverculitis (c) Hypoacidity (d) Atonic ulcer

158. Hydrochloric acid, which is one of the digestive juices, corrodes the walls of the stomach and duodenum to produce:
(a) Dysentery (b) Peptic ulcer (c) Gastrasthenia (d) Gastradenitis

159. Tobacco users and people suffering from mental tension are prone to:
(a) Peritonitis (b) Gastralgia (c) Gastorrhagia (d) Peptic ulcer

160. Patients who are bedridden develop bedsores which are medically known as:
(a) Adherent ulcer (b) Decubitus ulcers (c) Endemic ulcer (d) Arterial ulcer

161. In patients suffering from which of the following disease do ulcers not heal easily?
    (a) Hypertension (b) Diabetes mellitus
    (c) Anaemia (d) Hypotension

162. Which of the following is seen in tobacco users?
    (a) Pallor (b) Hypoacidity (c) Hyperacidity
    (d) Impaired kidney function

Malaria

163. In which of the following countries is malaria prevalent?
    (a) Asia (b) Antarctica (c) Australia (d) China

164. Which insect harbours the malaria parasites?
    (a) Sand fly (b) Anopheles mosquito (c) Culex mosquito (d) Common fly

165. How is malaria transmitted?
    (a) Through infected needles (b) Through blood transfusion (c) Through mosquito bites (d) Through contaminated food or water

166. For which disease are these parasites responsible: P. vivax, P. malariae, P. ovale and P. falciparum?
    (a) Filaria (b) Malaria (c) Encephalitis (d) Meningitis

Burns

167. Which part of the skin is affected in first-degree burns?
    (a) Upper layer of epidermis (b) Complete epidermis (c) Stratum papillare (d) Stratum reticulare

168. In which type of burns part of the epidermis and dermis are destroyed?
    (a) First-degree burns (b) Second-degree burns
    (c) Electrical burns (d) Both (a) and (c)

169. In which type of burns are the epidermis and dermis destroyed?
    (a) Dilute acid burns (b) Dilute alkali burns
    (c) Third-degree burns (d) Hot water burns

Cardiovascular diseases

170. When there is a deviation of the rhythm of the heart from the normal rhythm, the condition is referred to as:
    (a) Arrythmiasis (b) Sclerosis (c) Diastole (d) Cardiocele

171. Which of the following is a heart disease?
    (a) Debility (b) Angina pectoris (c) Epilepsy (d) Catabolism

172. Sometimes the veins become dilated and the heart valves do not function properly. This may result in reversing the blood flow. What is this condition known as?
    (a) Arteritis (b) Gardner's syndrome (c) Arteriomalacia (d) Varicose veins

173. When there is clotting of blood in the blood vessels, it is known as:
    (a) Dyscrasia (b) Thrombosis (c) Hemokoniosis (d) Arteriorrhagia

174. The heart is nourished by the right and left coronary arteries. If the coronary artery gets blocked then the heart will receive less blood. What is this condition known as?
    (a) Ischaemia (b) Hypertension (c) Hypotension (d) Cardioplegia

Diseases of the skin

175. When the scalp and hair become infested with lice, the condition is known as:
    (a) Myocardosis (b) Pediculosis (c) Necrosis (d) Paridrosis

176. An infection that forms round, itchy lesions on the skin is known as:
    (a) Ringworms (b) Eczema (c) Rash (d) Herpes

177. Sarcoptes scabei is a parasite that causes an itchy skin disease. What is the disease known as?
    (a) Chilblain (b) Scabies (c) Dermathemia (d) Eczema

178. A type of eczema that occurs as a result of handling flour or sugar is known as:
(a) Impetigo (b) Hiemalis dermatitis (c) Grocer's itch (d) Dermatoconiosis

179. In which of the following diseases does the outer layer of the skin renew itself much faster than in normal human skin?
(a) Psoriasis (b) Vitiligo (c) Dermatobiasis (d) Leprosy

180. Which of the following diseases results from faulty pigmentation of the skin?
(a) Eczema (b) Leukoderma (c) Dandruff (d) Dermatitis

181. In which of the following is there an allergic reaction on the skin?
(a) Pick's syndrome (b) Meningitis (c) Rhinitis (d) Wilson's disease

182. Herpes is a skin disease, the cause of which is:
(a) A bacillus (b) A virus (c) An insect (d) Mosquito

183. Which type of disease is ringworm categorized as?
(a) Viral disease (b) Bacterial disease (c) Fungal disease (d) Both (a) and (b)

Encephalitis

184. Of which part of the body is there inflammation in encephalitis?
(a) Lungs (b) Brain (c) Heart (d) Liver

185. Which of the following is responsible for transmitting encephalitis?
(a) Rats (b) Dogs (c) Mosquitoes (d) Flies

186. Which of the following cause encephalitis?
(a) Only bacteria (b) Mainly virus but also bacteria (c) Polluted water (d) Fungus

187. Which of the following is the carrier of the encephalitis virus?
(a) Culex mosquito (b) Anopheles mosquito (c) Aedes albopictus (d) A. variegatus

188. Which bacterium causes typhoid?
     (a) Salmonella typhi (b) B. typhosus (c) B. botulinus (d) B. tetani

189. How is typhoid transmitted?
     (a) Touch (b) Contaminated food or water (c) Body fluids (d) Air

190. A kind of paralysis that is accompanied by tremor of the limbs and associated with reduced dopamine in the tissues of the brain is known as:
     (a) Parkinson's disease (b) Paralysis (c) Polio-myelitis (d) Paralytic stroke

191. In which disease does inflammation take place of the membrane surrounding the spinal chord and the brain?
     (a) Microcephaly (b) Meningitis (c) Spondylitis (d) Glioma

192. In which of the following diseases does inflammation of the lungs occur?
     (a) Pneumonia (b) Pott's disease (c) Bronchitis (d) Pneumomalacia

193. In which of the following diseases does the tonsil become swollen?
     (a) Parotitis (b) Pharyngitis (c) Tonsillitis (d) Laryngitis

194. When certain portions of the tissues of the body die, it is referred to as:
     (a) Paralysis (b) Bed sores (c) Gangrene (d) Paraplegia

195. What does one mean by alopecia?
     (a) Baldness (b) Skin allergy (c) Obesity (d) Excess growth of hair

196. Plague is a highly infectious disease that is transmitted by:
     (a) Cats (b) Rats (c) Dogs (d) Cows

197. Which is the disease in which the body is unable to use iron to synthesize haemoglobin, thereby leading to severe anaemia?

(a) Thalassaemia (b) Haemolysis (c) Haemophilia
(d) Haemoptysis

198. What is the other name for German measles?
(a) Scarlet fever (b) Rubella (c) Herpes
(d) Mazern

199. In which of the following does the tongue become swollen?
(a) Glossitis (b) Psoriasis (c) Chilblain (d) Leukoderma

200. What is the terminology used to describe excess glucose in the blood?
(a) Hyperglycaemia (b) Hypoglycaemia (c) Hyper-
tension (d) Hypotension

201. When a person excessively worries about his illnesses or imagines being inflicted with illness, he is said to be suffering from:
(a) Hysteria (b) Agromania (c) Depression
(d) Hypochondria

202. What is chancroid?
(a) Tonsillitis (b) Fever (c) Paratyphoid
(d) Venereal disease

203. Which of the following is a venereal disease?
(a) Gonorrhoea (b) Cervical cancer (c) Urinary
calculi (d) Granulitis

204. In which of the following diseases does inflammation of the colon occur?
(a) Duodenal ulcer (b) Gastric ulcer (c) Colitis
(d) Piles

205. Inflammation of the mouth takes place in:
(a) Glossitis (b) Stomatitis (c) Halitosis (d) Tonsillitis

206. In which of the following diseases are the thyroid glands enlarged?
(a) Goitre (b) AIDS (c) Laryngitis (d) Pharyngitis

207. In which of the following diseases is there pain and inflammation of the joints in the body?
(a) Osteomalacia (b) Arthritis (c) Achondroplasia
(d) Arthrogryposis

208. A disease that is accompanied by fever and causes damage to the liver and spleen is known as:
(a) Ascites (b) Kala-azar (c) Splenic abscess (d) Gastroenteritis

209. The parasite Laishmann Donovan is responsible for causing:
(a) Kala-azar (b) Yellow fever (c) Filaria (d) Oncocerciasis

210. Which of the following is the carrier of Laishmann Donovan?
(a) Common fly (b) Black fly (c) Tsetse fly (d) Sand fly

211. Which of the following is responsible for influenza?
(a) Virus (b) Fly (c) Mosquito (d) Bacteria

212. Earlier it was thought that influenza was caused by:
(a) Bacillus abortus (b) Bacillus pyogenes (c) Hemophilus influenza (d) Bacillus albuminis

213. Which is the site of attack of the influenza virus?
(a) Stomach (b) Brain (c) Liver (d) Respiratory tract

214. Passing of frequent, watery motions is known as:
(a) Constipation (b) Tarry stools (c) Diarrhoea (d) Scybala

215. Over-eating or infection from food or water is responsible for:
(a) Nephritis (b) Colitis (c) Gastric ulcer (d) Diarrhoea

216. Which among the following is caused by Rickettsia rickettsii, a microorganism?
(a) Rocky Mountain spotted fever (b) Rickets (c) Scarlet fever (d) Mediterranean fever

217. Which of the following is a chronic and acute kidney disease?
(a) Trachitis (b) Nephritis (c) Gastritis (d) Peritonitis

218. Toxaemia resulting from the retention of poisonous waste material in the blood stream is known as:
(a) Leukaemia (b) Hematochyluria (c) Erythroblastoma (d) Uraemia

219. Which disease does STD refer to?
(a) Sexually transmitted disease (b) Standard transmitted disease (c) Staphylococcus transmitted diseases (d) Streptococcus transmitted diseases

220. What happens in rhinitis?
(a) The ear is swollen (b) The mouth is swollen (c) The tongue is swollen (d) The nasal mucous membrane is swollen

221. An infectious disease brought about by a virus causing swelling and pain in the salivary glands is known as:
(a) Mumps (b) Parotidoscirrhus (c) Tonsillitis (d) Metastatic parotitis

222. A fly is responsible for spreading the disease trypanosomiasis or sleeping sickness. Which is this fly?
(a) Sand fly (b) Tsetse fly (c) Common fly (d) Black fly

223. The differentiating power of the body's immune system is reduced with age. In consequence, it fails to differentiate between disease germs and body's own tissues. As a result, it attacks body's own tissues by mistake producing auto-immune diseases. Which of the following is thought to be an auto-immune disease?
(a) Cancer (b) Parkinson's disease (c) Rheumatoid arthritis (d) Colitis

224. In which of the following diseases occur problems of the heart muscles from lack of selenium?
(a) Cardiagra (b) Keshan disease (c) Cardialgia (d) Cardianeuria

225. Which of the following diseases is associated with the inflammation of the kidneys?

(a) Pott's disease (b) Richter's hernia (c) Bright's disease (d) Rheumatism

226. In a particular type of malaria the patient's urine changes to a dark colour as a result of the red blood cells getting ruined. Which one of the following is this malaria?
(a) Black-water fever (b) Filaria (c) Malarial neuralgia (d) Dengue

227. Lack of hormones produced by the adrenal glands leads to a disease known as:
(a) Pellagra (b) Conn's syndrome (c) Scurvy (d) Addison's disease

228. Malfunctioning of which gland leads to improper physical and mental growth?
(a) Adrenal (b) Thyroid (c) Pancreas (d) Lymphatic

229. What is the other name for Bright's disease?
(a) Osteomyelitis (b) Poliomyelitis (c) Nephritis (d) Peritonitis

230. Poisonous gases like hydrogen sulfide, hydrocyanic acid, carbon monoxide and carcinogens are present in cigarette smoke. They cause:
(a) Dyspnoea (b) Sore throat, cancer (c) Cardialgia (d) Cardiasthenia

231. In which of the following diseases are the intestines and stomach affected?
(a) Peritendinitis (b) Giardiasis (c) Gastritis (d) Gastroenteritis

232. Which of the following parts of the body is affected in Gardner's syndrome?
(a) Stomach (b) Brain (c) Liver (d) Colon

233. Which of the following is a genetic disorder?
(a) Leukosis (b) Albinism (c) Leukoplakia (d) Laloplegia

234. Absence of which enzyme causes albinism?
(a) Tyrosinase (b) Amylase (c) Protease (d) Lipase

235. In which of the following diseases do liver problems arise?

(a) Leukopenia (b) Tyrosinemia (c) Mumps (d) Mastoiditis

236. In which of the following diseases does the haemoglobin molecule show a change?
(a) Rubella (b) Smallpox (c) Metritis (d) Sickle-cell anaemia

237. In which disease is the spleen affected?
(a) Metrocele (b) Gaucher's disease (c) Pelioma (d) Gastrorrhoea

238. In which of the following diseases is the blood supply to an area of the brain interrupted?
(a) Stroke (b) Down's syndrome (c) Parkinson's disease (d) Multiple sclerosis

239. In which of the following diseases does the blood not clot?
(a) Anaemia (b) Haemophilia (c) Pernicious anaemia (d) Haemoglobinemia

240. Which of the following is a genetic disease?
(a) Haemophilia (b) Rickets (c) Rubella (d) Rhinitis

241. In which disease does the abdominal cavity get filled with fluid?
(a) Hepatitis (b) Hernia (c) Septicaemia (d) Ascites

242. The expanding of an artery leads to a weak and swollen area and is known as:
(a) Rhinoantritis (b) Aneurysm (c) Arteriasis (d) Arteriectopia

243. In which of the following is there headache on one side of the head?
(a) Sinusitis (b) Influenza (c) Migraine (d) Ophthalmic trouble

244. In ottis media which part of the body is affected?
(a) Eyes (b) Ear (c) Mouth (d) Nose

245. A disease of the lungs is common among potters from breathing in of dust. Which is this disease?
(a) Potter's asthma (b) Hay fever (c) Renal asthma (d) Tuberculosis

246. What does the term Oariopathy refer to?
    (a) Heart disease (b) Ovarian disease (c) Lung disease (d) Brain disorder
247. In which of the following does the stomach become paralysed?
    (a) Gastroparalysis (b) Gastralgia (c) Ascites (d) Gastric ulcer
248. Which of the following leads to diabetes mellitus?
    (a) Lack of blood (b) Lack of iron (c) Lack of insulin (d) Lack of calcium
249. Yellow fever is an infectious disease prevalent in Africa and is caused by a virus which is carried by a certain mosquito. Which mosquito is responsible for this?
    (a) Anopheles (b) Culex (c) Aedes egypti (d) Theobaldia annulata

3
SYMPTOMS OF DISEASES

Infections
250. Occurrence of fever, along with shivering, headache and bodyache, with the fever subsiding and returning again, are symptoms of which disease?
    (a) Malaria (b) Influenza (c) Scarlet fever (d) Hay fever
251. Acute diarrhoea and vomiting leading to dehydration are symptoms of which disease?
    (a) Giardiasis (b) Cholera (c) Typhoid (d) Paratyphoid
252. An insensitive patch on the skin, followed by disfigurement of hands, feet, face, etc., are symptoms associated with which disease?
    (a) Leprosy (b) Vitiligo (c) Psoriasis (d) Eczema

253. Malaria parasites not only destroy the red blood cells but also leave behind their excreta. This is responsible for:

(a) Weakness (b) Headache (c) Anorexia (d) Fever and the feeling of cold with shivering

254. Repetition of the malaria fever in cycles is due to:

(a) Total non-destruction of malaria parasites
(b) Incomplete destruction of malaria parasites
(c) Improper diet (d) Weakness

255. Nausea, diarrhoea and vomiting are symptoms of:

(a) Duodenal ulcer (b) Hyperacidity (c) Gastric ulcer (d) Food poisoning

256. Pain and swelling of the salivary glands along with headache and fever are symptoms of which disease?

(a) Mumps (b) Pharyngitis (c) Measles (d) Bronchitis

257. Cough, loss of weight and fever are some of the symptoms of:

(a) Influenza (b) Tuberculosis (c) Tonsillitis (d) Sore throat

258. Bodyache, headache, sore throat, cough, fever, and watering of eyes may suggest an attack of:

(a) Measles (b) Influenza (c) Typhoid (d) Malaria

259. Headache and fever along with vesicles containing fluid may be the symptoms of:

(a) Syphilis (b) Chicken pox (c) Rubella (d) Measles

260. In which of the following do symptoms of fever, sore throat, constipation, nausea, etc., show up?

(a) Tonsillitis (b) Helminthiasis (c) Typhoid (d) Dyspepsia

261. In which of the following diseases does a membrane develop covering the pharynx and tonsils, causing difficulty in breathing and swallowing?

(a) Tonsillitis (b) Diphtheria (c) Pharyngitis
(d) Rhinitis

Neoplasms

262. With which disease are the symptoms of non-healing ulcer, prolonged cough, hoarseness, difficulty in swallowing and loss in weight associated?
(a) Decubitus ulcer (b) Laryngitis (c) Cancer
(d) Pharyngitis

263. For which of the following diseases can symptoms like headache, disturbances in vision, nausea and a feeling of dizziness arise?
(a) Hypotension (b) Sinusitis (c) Migraine
(d) Brain tumour (Glioma)

264. Long-drawn diarrhoea, passage of blood in the stool, anaemia or any other sudden change in the bowel habit of a person needs medical attention, for it may be indicative of:
(a) Food poisoning (b) Giardiasis (c) Cholera
(d) Bowel cancer

265. In which disease do symptoms of fever, anaemia, a painful throat, feeling of weakness and weariness, etc., manifest themselves?
(a) Pharyngorhinitis (b) Influenza (c) Herpetic tonsillitis (d) Leukaemia

266. Which of the following may hoarseness of voice be the symptom of?
(a) Goitre (b) Tumour affecting the vocal cord
(c) Pharyngoplegia (d) Laryngismus

267. In which of the following diseases do the lymph nodes become large?
(a) Bright's disease (b) Lymphocythenia
(c) Hodgkin's disease (d) Lymphocytopenia

Miscellaneous

268. A pain in the top part of the stomach, specially when it is empty, may be due to which of the following?

(a) Peptic ulcer (b) Dysentery (c) Food poisoning (d) Appendicitis

269. If the tongue is swollen and if the facial skin and the skin of the hands, etc., become red, it may be indicative of:
(a) Scleroderma (b) Pellagra (c) Eczema (d) Rash

270. The simultaneous occurrence of different diseases like diarrhoea, fever, pneumonia, cancer, etc., are the symptoms of:
(a) AIDS (b) Debility (c) Breast cancer (d) Hodgkin's disease

271. A severe cardiac pain which may be of a temporary nature and which may spread to the arms may be due to:
(a) Angina Pectoris (b) Bronchitis (c) Bucardia (d) Myocarditis

272. What are the common symptoms of giardiasis?
(a) Persistent stomach ache (b) Prolonged diarrhoea (c) Black stool (d) Indigestion

273. Soreness of throat, stiffness of neck, headache, vomiting and fever may indicate an attack of:
(a) Meningitis (b) Malaria (c) Tonsillitis (d) Bronchitis

274. Sudden fractures in old people may indicate:
(a) Rheumatism (b) Osteoporosis (c) Arthritis (d) Parkinson's disease

275. Deposition of bilirubin gives a yellowish look to patients suffering from:
(a) Hepatalgia (b) Hepatargy (c) Jaundice (d) Hepatauxe

276. When a person sees double objects when actually it is single, it indicates that he may be suffering from:
(a) Photophobia (b) Diplopia (c) Myopia (d) Astigmatism

277. Softness and pain in the lower right side of abdomen along with symptoms of nausea and vomiting may be due to:

(a) Appendicitis (b) Indigestion (c) Gastric ulcer (d) Hyperacidity

278. Itching, swelling, and reddish coloration of the skin from some form of allergy may be the symptoms of:
(a) Ringworm (b) Eczema (c) Scleroderma (d) Ichthyosis

279. Development of sores between the toes and fingers, accompanied by itching, may be the result of the skin infection:
(a) Scabies (b) Leprosy (c) Psoriasis (d) Vitiligo

280. Loss in weight, feeling of hunger, and thirst, along with frequent bouts of urination, are the signs of a particular disease. Which disease is it?
(a) Hypertension (b) Diabetes (c) Hypotension (d) Rabies

281. Abdominal pain that occurs some hours after eating food, and lessens on eating again, are the symptoms of which disease?
(a) Duodenal ulcer (b) Colitis (c) Dyspepsia (d) Kidney damage

282. A heavy feeling in the stomach, heartburn, and pain in the top part of the abdomen may be due to:
(a) Hepatitis (b) Indigestion (c) Gallstone (d) Appendicitis

283. Which disease is indicated by fits in which the teeth are set firmly together and there are twitchy movements of the hands, legs, and muscles of the face, followed by unconsciousness?
(a) Meningitis (b) Glioma (c) Parkinson's disease (d) Epilepsy

284. In which of the following does the patient lose control over his muscles and exhibits tremors?
(a) Arthritis (b) Parkinson's disease (c) Rheumatism (d) Kinesalgia

285. Prolonged diarrhoea with pus-filled and bloody stools may be the symptoms of:

42

(a) Fatty diarrhoea (b) Summer diarrhoea (c) Ulcerative colitis (d) Green diarrhoea

286. In which of the following diseases does a patient have fever accompanied by cough and a pain in the chest?
(a) Tonsillitis (b) Bronchitis (c) Laryngitis (d) Pharyngitis

287. When the body is under foreign invasion by germs, the number of white blood cells in the blood increases, thereby indicating infection in a blood test. What are these white blood cells known as?
(a) Leucocytes (b) Erythrocytes (c) Plasma (d) Thrombocytes

288. In which of the following diseases does the eosinophil count increase considerably in a blood test?
(a) Worm infestation (b) Asthma (c) Both (a) and (b) (d) Hypertension

289. In certain diseases the number of white blood corpuscles plunges below the normal limit. What is this condition known as?
(a) Leukaemia (b) Leucopenia (c) Leukocyturia (d) Leukocytosis

290. Sores near the angles of the mouth and a swollen red tongue are the symptoms of which deficiency?
(a) Riboflavin (b) Pyridoxin (c) Vitamin C (d) Vitamin B_{12}

291. Stiffness of neck, mental disturbance, high temperature, headache and coma are some of the symptoms manifested in which of the following diseases?
(a) Encephalitis (b) Cerebralgia (c) Delirium (d) Epilepsy

292. Blocked nose, sneezing, watery fluid coming out of the nose are some of the symptoms accompanying which disease?
(a) Tuberculosis (b) Rhinitis (c) Parotitis (d) Kala-azar

293. Fever with severe joint pains may be indicative of
(a) Arthritis (b) Rheumatic fever (c) Arthalgia
(d) Influenza

294. Lockjaw, in which the patient finds difficulty in
opening his mouth, is the symptom of which
disease?
(a) Tetanus (b) Stomatitis (c) Oral cancer (d) Gingivitis

295. In Addison's disease the body becomes darker in
colour. To which of the following is this due to?
(a) More salt depositing on skin (b) More fat
depositing on skin (c) More melanin depositing
on skin (d) Increase of haemoglobin in blood

296. The reddish appearance of the pharynx along
with a dry cough may be the symptoms of:
(a) Pharyngitis (b) Bronchitis (c) Pleurisy
(d) Tuberculosis

297. When the longing to eat food is lacking, what is
it known as?
(a) Dyspnoea (b) Dyspepsia (c) Anorexia
(d) Anorrhorrhea

298. A deficiency of thiamine in the body will lead to:
(a) Hypertension (b) Anorexia (c) Diabetes
(d) Hypotension

299. Difficulty in breathing is a common complaint of
heart patients. What is the other name for it?
(a) Oedema (b) Aneurysm (c) Angina pectoris
(d) Dyspnoea

300. Patients suffering from San Joaquin fever exhibit:
(a) Indigestion (b) Respiratory trouble (c) Hyperacidity (d) Heart trouble

301. Hoarseness and weariness of voice are the common
symptoms of:
(a) Stomatitis (b) Gingivitis (c) Laryngitis
(d) Goitre

302. Albinism exhibits white skin, white hair, etc. This
is due to:

(a) Excess of melanin (b) Absence of melanin (c) Excess sugar (d) Less calcium

303. In which of the following diseases are there symptoms of kidney damage and formation of cataracts?
(a) Hypertension (b) Hypercalcaemia (c) Galactosemia (d) Hypotension

304. In which of the following diseases symptoms of severe digestive problems and bronchial problems are exhibited?
(a) Bronchitis (b) Colitis (c) Gastric ulcer (d) Cystic fibrosis

305. The abdomen increases in size in patients suffering from:
(a) Ascites (b) Rabies (c) Gastric ulcer (d) Jaundice

306. In which disease is pain in joints manifested?
(a) Osteotabes (b) Arthritis (c) Osteorrhagia (d) Varicose veins

307. Hyperacidity, i.e., excessive acid in the stomach is a symptom of:
(a) Kidney trouble (b) Achlorhydria (c) Peptic ulcer (d) Acute hepatitis

308. Which of the following is a symptom of emphysema?
(a) Difficult breathing (b) Stomach ache (c) Headache (d) Indigestion

4

PREVENTION OF DISEASES

Diseases

309. How can one prevent angina pectoris?
(a) By taking a diet containing less vitamins (b) By taking a diet containing less cholesterol and fat (c) By taking a diet containing more salt (d) Consuming less sugar

310. Eating food with a high fibre content helps prevent:
(a) Gastric ulcer (b) Indigestion (c) Diabetes (d) Colon cancer

311. Because of the high fibre content in the food they eat, the prevalence of colon cancer is less among:
(a) Vegetarians (b) Predominantly egg eaters (c) Predominantly meat eaters (d) Predominantly smoked fish eaters

312. Food should be properly cooked and eaten; otherwise there are chances of:
(a) Salmonella food poisoning (b) Dyspepsia (c) Gastric ulcer (d) Duodenal ulcer

313. Diseased birds should not be eaten, for that will lead to:
(a) Colon cancer (b) Duodenal ulcer (c) Stomach cancer (d) Food poisoning

314. It has been found that the incidence of heart attack is low amongst Japanese fishermen because of their high consumption of:
(a) Mutton (b) Fish (c) Beef (d) Pork

315. Disposable syringes, needles, and gloves are recommended for prevention of the spread of:
(a) AIDS (b) Cancer (c) Leprosy (d) Tuberculosis

316. Linen of AIDS patients is washed thoroughly to kill all AIDS germs. Which method is recommended?
(a) Washing with dettol (b) Washing with soap and water (c) Washing with hot water, soap and bleaching powder (d) Washing with Teepol.

317. Needles, syringes, etc., used for taking blood samples from AIDS patients should be subjected to which of the following?
(a) Thrown into a closed dustbin (b) Burnt (c) Dipped in dettol solution (d) Washed with soap and water

318. 'Doctors and nurses should wear gloves and have no cuts on their hands.' This precaution is taken against which disease?
(a) Encephalitis (b) Meningitis (c) Cholera (d) AIDS

319. Personal cleanliness and cleanliness of the surroundings are vital for avoiding:
(a) Food poisoning (b) Pleurisy (c) Filaria (d) Tuberculosis

320. All fruits and vegetables brought from the market should be thoroughly washed before cooking or eating, because:
(a) Washing makes them easier to cook (b) They may have disease germs and pesticide residues on them. (c) Washing removes any artificial colour (d) Both (a) and (c)

321. Hands should be washed thoroughly before cooking or eating to avoid:
(a) Gingivitis (b) Dentalgia (c) Infection (d) Indigestion

322. Why do people working in the kitchen of hotels and restaurants wear a cap?
(a) To prevent food from being contaminated by hair (b) To prevent the hair from drying up through heat (c) To protect the head from heat (d) To protect the head from fumes generated during cooking

323. The incidence of cervical cancer in women can be lessened if they have a regular check-up which is done by:
(a) Cervical cytology (b) Cervimeter (c) Skiagraphy (d) Uterometer

324. Which of the following must one eat in order to lessen the occurrence of cardio-vascular diseases?
(a) Saturated fats of animal origin (b) Unsaturated fats of vegetable origin (c) A diet rich in sugar and salt (d) A diet rich in red meat

325. Which of the following diseases has been found to be associated with homosexuals, drug addicts, promiscuous persons and haemophilics?
(a) Syphilis (b) AIDS (c) Leprosy (d) Gonorrhoea

326. Bodies of AIDS patients should be handled with proper precaution. Why?
(a) Because the AIDS virus continues to be active in the patient's blood for some period after death.
(b) Because the body emits a foul odour (c) Because the body becomes stiff and may be damaged (d) Because the body decomposes fast and therefore handling becomes difficult

327. Bodies are preserved by injecting them with formalin. The process is known as embalming. Why is it necessary for doctors and others to take extra precaution while embalming the body of an AIDS victim?
(a) Because the air surrounding the patient's body is contaminated with the AIDS virus (b) Because the surface of the patient's body may be covered with the virus (c) To avoid infection from the blood and fluids coming out of the victim's body while embalming (d) Because touching the patient may cause AIDS

Diet

328. Serum cholesterol may increase in a person taking:
(a) Too much coffee (b) Too much salt (c) Too much fruit juice (d) Too much sugar

329. Caffeine is the harmful factor present in:
(a) Beer (b) Wine (c) Coffee (d) Whisky

330. A diet with less salt is necessary for patients suffering from:
(a) Hypotension (b) Jaundice (c) Hypertension (d) Peptic ulcer

331. Which type of diet should be eaten to lessen the chances of a heart attack?

(a) Vegetarian diet (b) Diet consisting of mutton (c) Diet consisting of eggs (d) Diet consisting of beef

332. Excess consumption of which of the following leads to an acute Vitamin B deficiency?
(a) Tea (b) Coffee (c) Coke (d) Alcohol

333. Excess alcoholism is not only harmful to health, but it may also cause loss of memory from the ailment known as:
(a) Paranoia (b) Wernicke's syndrome (c) Addison's disease (d) Korsakoff's syndrome

334. Regular exercise and a diet with enough calcium and Vitamin D should be taken in order to avoid the weakening and destruction of bones in old age. Which is this disease?
(a) Epiphysitis (b) Osteoporosis (c) Rickets (d) Hypercalcaemia

335. Coffee, tea, cocoa, alcohol, spicy food, and oily food cause acid secretion, and therefore, should be avoided by patients suffering from:
(a) Gastric ulcer (b) Diabetes (c) Cancer (d) Hypotension

336. The large number of factories have increased pollution tremendously. Lead accumulates in the bones and soft tissues. The toxic effects of stored lead have been found to be reduced by:
(a) Protein-rich diet (b) Calcium-rich diet (c) Vitamin-rich diet (d) Fibre-rich diet

337. Children should be given food with enough calcium and Vitamin D in order to avoid:
(a) Rickets (b) Osteocarcinoma (c) Poliomyelitis (d) Ostemia

338. Green leafy vegetables, raisins, dates, eggs, jaggery and meat are rich in iron and should be given to growing children. Which disease is prevented by including these in the diet?
(a) Thalassaemia (b) Anaemia (c) Sickle-cell anaemia (d) Haemophilia

339. A patient afflicted with which of the following diseases should thrive on a low-tyrosine diet?
(a) Xeroderma (b) Hypertension (c) Tyrosinemia (d) Down's syndrome

340. In order to avoid indigestion which of the following should be included in the diet?
(a) Grapes (b) Cabbages (c) Radishes (d) Bengal gram

341. Too many cups of strong tea and coffee should not be taken in order to avoid:
(a) Gastroenteritis (b) Peptic ulcer (c) Gastradynia (d) Colitis

342. Children should not only avoid eating too many sweets, but also brush their teeth after eating sweets in order to avoid:
(a) Rigg's disease (b) Halitosis (c) Dental caries (d) Dentinoid

Vaccines

343. As protection against tuberculosis which vaccination should be taken?
(a) BCG (b) Triple antigen (c) Double antigen (d) MMR

344. Recently, two Indian scientists reported a new vaccine against rabies. The two scientists are R. Selvakumar and T. Jacob John from Vellore. What is the name of this vaccine?
(a) Rabipur (b) DPT (c) Sabin vaccine (d) Rabies vaccine

345. Diphtheria toxoid is used as a prevention against diphtheria. What is it?
(a) A vaccine (b) A tablet (c) A capsule (d) A tonic

346. An oral dose of vaccine is usually given to children to protect them against poliomyelitis. What is it known as?
(a) Autogenous vaccine (b) Sabin vaccine (c) BCG vaccine (d) Salk vaccine

347. All people who keep dogs should get them vaccinated in order to prevent them from developing:
(a) Caries (b) Lice (c) Rabies (d) Ticks

348. A vaccination that gives protection against typhoid and paratyphoid for some period is known as:
(a) Haffkine's vaccine (b) Jennerian vaccination (c) BCG (d) TAB vaccine

349. Which of the following gives protection against tetanus?
(a) TABC (b) MMR (c) Tetanus toxoid (d) Humanized vaccine

350. Poliomyelitis can also be prevented by injecting a certain vaccine. Which is this vaccine?
(a) Wright's vaccine (b) Salk vaccine (c) Haffkine's prophylactic fluid (d) Bacillus Calmette-Guerin vaccine

351. An attack of influenza can be prevented by which of the following methods?
(a) Getting vaccinated (b) Taking preventive medicines (c) Taking Vitamin A (d) Taking Vitamin D

Miscellaneous
352. Eating at proper intervals, not keeping the stomach empty for long hours, avoiding the consumption of tobacco, and avoiding mental tension are some of the precautions one can take to avoid:
(a) Achlorhydria (b) Peptic ulcer (c) Bowel cancer (d) Stomach cancer

353. The foetus may be harmed if a pregnant woman takes many cups of:
(a) Lemon juice (b) Coffee (c) Carrot juice (d) Orange juice

354. It has been reported that Reye's syndrome can be prevented in children suffering from influenza or chicken-pox if they are not treated with a particular drug. Which is that drug?

51

(a) Analgin (b) Paracetamol (c) Aspirin (d) Penicillin

355. There is a fish that feeds on mosquito larvae and destroys mosquito breeding sites. Which is this fish?
(a) Salmon (b) Gambusia (c) Herring (d) Hilsa

356. Which of the following has been found to attack the larvae of mosquitoes and hence can substitute insecticides?
(a) Bacillus thuringiensis H 14 (b) B. subtilis (c) Bacillus saprogenes (d) Bacillus utpadel

357. Until now insecticides are in use to kill mosquitoes. Now a fungus has been found by Dr. Tom Sweeney to kill mosquitoes. Which is this fungus?
(a) Culicinomyces (b) Phycomycetes (c) Penicillium notatum (d) Aspergillus flavus

358. Why is it not advisable for a pregnant woman to go in for X-rays?
(a) Because the skin becomes dry (b) Because X-rays produce vitamin deficiency (c) Because the cells of the foetus may be harmed by the ionising radiation (d) Because X-rays produce protein deficiency

359. Milk is heated to kill pathogenic bacteria. What is this process known as?
(a) Sterilization (b) Pasteurization (c) Pasteur treatment (d) Fermentation

360. Which of the following should be adopted to keep the heart and lungs in order and reduce body fat?
(a) Regular intake of food rich in calories and proteins (b) Regular exercises (c) Regular intake of Vitamin A (d) Regular intake of glucose

361. Persons suffering from high blood pressure should not subject themselves to excessive physical exertion and mental excitation in order to avoid:
(a) Stroke (b) Thrombosis (c) Angina pectoris (d) Chorea

362. The statutory warning on a cigarette packet reads 'CIGARETTE SMOKING IS INJURIOUS TO HEALTH'. Still many people resort to smoking. Which of the following diseases victimises many a smoker?
(a) Chronic bronchitis (b) Tuberculosis (c) Pulmonitis (d) Pleurocele

363. When a person has to visit a malaria-infested area the doctor puts him on a particular drug as a preventive measure. Which is that drug?
(a) Analgin (b) Aspirin (c) Paracetamol (d) Chloroquine

364. Which of the following should be avoided to keep high blood pressure at bay?
(a) Tea (b) Exercise (c) Stress (d) Fatigue

365. What should an influenza patient do in order to avoid transmitting the influenza virus to other people?
(a) Go outdoors (b) Stay at home (c) Disinfect the water (d) Fumigate the house.

366. Which of the following has been found to be associated with women who resort to smoking?
(a) Headaches (b) Bodyaches (c) Skin problems (d) Infertility and abortion

5
DRUGS

General Information

367. A drug that can be bought from a chemist's shop without a doctor's prescription is known as:
(a) BTC drug (b) OTC drug (c) ATC drug (d) AOTC drug

368. An injectable has to satisfy one of the following conditions. Which is it?
(a) Sterile (b) Alcoholic (c) Viscous (d) Non-irritant

369. Different companies sell the same drug under different names. What are these names known as?
(a) IUPAC name (b) Nomenclature (c) Company's name (d) Trade name

370. Which of the following is used in Nuclear Medicine?
(a) DNA (b) RNA (c) Enzymes (d) Radio-isotopes

371. After an illness which of the following is given by a doctor for fast recovery?
(a) Anthelmintic (b) Antiemetic (c) Analeptic (d) Analgesic

372. Which of the following induces vomiting?
(a) An antipyretic (b) An antiemetic (c) An emetic (d) Cathartic

373. Which of the following drugs is used for deworming?
(a) Anthelmintic (b) Hormones (c) Steroids (d) Antibacterial

374. What is a medicine that increases sweating known as?
(a) Antihidrotic (b) Diaphoretic (c) Depurant (d) Astringent

375. What is the function of a purgative?
(a) To empty the bowels (b) To empty the duodenum (c) To empty the stomach (d) To empty the kidneys

376. How is insulin generally administered to diabetic patients?
(a) Injection (b) Tablet (c) Capsule (d) Syrup

377. Medicines which are used to bring down acidity are known as:
(a) Analeptics (b) Antacids (c) Digestants (d) Anabolic Steroids

Analgesics and Antipyretics
378. What is the drug that reduces the temperature of the body known as?

54

(a) Analgesic (b) Antipyretic (c) Antiemetic
(d) Anodyne

379. What is a pain-killer known as?
(a) Analgesic (b) Anaesthetic (c) Antispasmodic
(d) Liniment

380. Which one of the following is the most common antipyretic drug?
(a) Ranitidine Hydrochloride (b) Penicillin
(c) Paracetamol (d) Salbutamol sulphate

381. Which one of the following is an analgesic?
(a) Ampicillin (b) Chloromycetin (c) Bacitracin
(d) Analgin

Anaesthetics

382. A drug that causes insensibility to pain is known as:
(a) Anaesthetic (b) Tranquillizer (c) Sedative
(d) Antaractic

383. A drug that brings about insensibility to the entire body and thus makes a patient unconscious is categorised as:
(a) Hypnotic (b) Neuroleptic (c) Local anaesthetic
(d) General anaesthetic

384. A drug that brings about insensibility only to the part of the body where it is applied is known as:
(a) Narcotic (b) Local anaesthetic (c) Barbiturate
(d) Muscle relaxant

385. Sir Humphrey Davy had suggested the name of a gas as an anaesthetic. Which one is it?
(a) Phosgene (b) Laughing gas (c) Carbon dioxide
(d) Carbon monoxide

386. Which one of the following is a local anaesthetic?
(a) Aspirin (b) Analgin (c) Orthocaine (d) Theophylline

387. One of the following chemical agents is used as a general anaesthetic. Which one is it?
(a) Trichloroethylene (b) Uracil (c) Ethambutol
(d) Tartar emetic

388. A cataract operation is usually carried out under:
(a) General anaesthesia (b) Local anaesthesia
(c) Without anaesthesia (d) Gwathmey's anaesthesia

389. One of the following is a local anaesthetic used in ointments. Which one is it?
(a) Testosterone (b) Naproxen (c) Benzocaine
(d) Lincomycin

390. During many operations one of the following drugs is used as a general anaesthetic. Which one is it?
(a) Thiopental (b) Trimethoprim (c) Minoxidil
(d) Clotrimazole

391. Which of the following is an anaesthetic that acts over a short duration?
(a) Metronidazole (b) Pentothal sodium
(c) Tinidazole (d) Chlorzoxazone

Antibacterials

392. Which of the following is a drug that kills or stops the growth of microorganisms?
(a) Analgesic (b) Anthelmintic (c) Antipyretic
(d) Antibiotic

393. From which of the following was Penicillin isolated?
(a) Penicillium notatum (b) Bacillus subtilis (c) Escherichia coli (d) Staphylococcus aureus

394. Against which of the following is Penicillin active?
(a) Diarrhoea (b) Diphtheria (c) Helminthiasis
(d) Colitis

395. From which of the following was streptomycin isolated?
(a) Micrococcus luteus (b) Streptomyces griseus
(c) Staphylococcus saprophyticus (d) Bacillus pumilus

396. Against which of the following was streptomycin found to be active?

56

(a) Migraine (b) Gingivitis (c) Tuberculosis
(d) Ringworm

397. Certain antibiotics are effective against many disease-causing microorganisms. What are they known as?
(a) Broad spectrum antibiotics (b) Bacteriostats (c) Specific antibiotics (d) Sulphonamides

398. What are the antibiotics that are effective against certain specific microorganisms known as?
(a) Broad spectrum antibiotics (b) Narrow spectrum antibiotics (c) Thin spectrum antibiotics (d) Weak spectrum antibiotics

399. What are antineoplastic antibiotics?
(a) Antibiotics that are used for the treatment of tuberculosis (b) Antibiotics that are used for the treatment of tonsillitis (c) Antibiotics that are used for the treatment of skin infections (d) Antibiotics that are used for the treatment of cancer

400. Which of the following is an antineoplastic antibiotic?
(a) Penicillin (b) Dactinomycin (c) Streptomycin (d) Chloramphenicol

401. Which of the following antibiotics is effective against tuberculosis?
(a) Penicillin (b) Erythromycin (c) Rifampicin (d) Chloramphenicol

402. Which of the following is a characteristic of all Penicillin group of antibiotics?
(a) β-lactam ring (b) Pyrrole ring (c) Benzene ring (d) Furan ring

403. To make it water-soluble so that it can be used for injections Penicillin is converted into:
(a) Calcium salt (b) Iron salt (c) Magnesium salt (d) Sodium or potassium salts

404. What are the antibiotics obtained from cephalosporium acremonium known as?
(a) Penicillins (b) Cephalosporins (c) Polyenes (d) β-lactam antibiotics

405. Against which of the following the antibiotics Neomycin and Gentamycin are used?
(a) Stomach infections (b) Throat infections (c) Skin infections (d) Tuberculosis

406. Which antibiotic is used in the treatment of typhoid and paratyphoid?
(a) Chloramphenicol (Chloromycetin) (b) Bacitracin (c) Penicillin (d) Ampicillin

407. From which of the following is Erythromycin isolated?
(a) Streptomyces griseus (b) Streptomyces erythreus (c) Streptomyces venezuelae (d) Penicillium notatum

408. Which of the following antibiotics is effective against ringworm?
(a) Ampicillin (b) Griseofulvin (c) Amoxycillin (d) Viomycin

409. 'Antibiotics should not be misused or irrationally used.' Why?
(a) Antibiotics are in short supply and therefore their misuse means further shortage (b) Misuse of antibiotics causes resistant strains of bacteria, so that the antibiotics become ineffective when used again (c) Wrong use may cause severe illness (d) Wrong use of antibiotics may cause damage to the body's immune system

410. Sulphonamides do not kill bacteria but stop their growth and multiplication. Which category do they fall in?
(a) Bactericide (b) Bacteriophage (c) Bacteriostatic (d) Antiviral

411. Sulphonamides are so called because they contain the sulphonamide group in their structure. Which of the following is the sulphonamide group?
(a) NH_2 (b) SO_2NH_2 (c) SO_3H (d) $CONH_2$

412. Which of the following drugs not having the 6-APA nucleus is used to control infection in surgical patients?

(a) Cephalosporins (b) Penicillin (c) Ampicillin
(d) Amoxycillin
413. Which of the following enzymes is produced by
bacteria to make penicillins ineffective?
(a) Ptyalin (b) Lacrimase (c) β-Lactamase
(d) Amylase

Antiallergics

414. Allergic manifestations have been associated with
the release of a chemical agent in the body. Which
is this chemical agent?
(a) Histamine (b) Histidine (c) Histaminase
(d) Hydrochloric acid
415. Drugs which reduce the effects of histamine and
thereby bring relief to allergic patients are known
as:
(a) Antiemetics (b) Antihistamines (c) Antipsoric
(d) Antiphlogistic
416. Which one of the following drugs is an antiallergic
drug?
(a) Analgin (b) Piperocaine (c) Phenargan
(d) Procaine
417. Benadryl is an antihistamine that is used in the
treatment of:
(a) Hay fever (b) Eczema (c) Rash (d) Insect bites
418. Which one of the following drugs may be used
to treat allergic manifestations in the eyes?
(a) Lasix (b) Antistine (c) Tinidazole (d) Heparin
419. Which of the following is an antihistaminic drug?
(a) Chlorpheniramine (b) Isoniazid (c) Cephalexin
(d) Aspirin

Antineoplastic drugs

420. What are antineoplastic drugs?
(a) Drugs that are used in the treatment of
meningitis (b) Drugs that are used in cancer
chemotherapy (c) Drugs that are used in the

treatment of encephalitis (d) Drugs that are used in the treatment of leprosy

421. In the treatment of which of the following diseases is the drug Procarbazine used?
(a) Hodgkin's disease (b) Breast cancer (c) Ovarian cancer (d) Prostatic carcinoma

422. The drug Vincristine Sulphate is used in the treatment of which of the following?
(a) Chordoma (b) Retinoblastoma (c) Choriocarcinoma (d) Lymphocytic Leukaemia

423. Methotrexate is used for treating children suffering from leukaemia. What is the other name for it?
(a) Amethopterin (b) Adenine (c) Metronidazole (d) Erythromycin

424. Which of the following drugs is used in the treatment of breast cancer?
(a) Mitotane (b) Busulphan (c) 5-Fluorouracil (d) Mithramycin

425. Which of the following drugs is used for treating patients suffering from myelocytic leukaemia?
(a) Thiotepa (b) Cytarabine (c) Ifosfamide (d) Cisplatin

426. Which of the following drugs is used for treating patients suffering from chronic lymphocytic leukaemia?
(a) Ethinyle stradiol (b) Tamoxifen citrate (c) Chlorambucil (d) Amoxycillin

427. Which of the following antibiotics is used in the treatment of Wilm's tumour?
(a) Dactinomycin (b) Penicillin (c) Streptomycin (d) Chloramphenicol

428. Which of the following drugs is used to treat cancer of the ovaries?
(a) Procaine (b) Hydroxyurea (c) Mercaptopurine (d) L-asparaginase

429. Which of the following is used in the treatment of cancer of the thyroid glands?

(a) Norfloxacin (b) Stilboestrol diphosphate (c) Radioiodine (d) Clavulanic acid

430. Vinblastin and Vincristine are antineoplastic drugs that have been isolated from a plant. Which plant is it?
(a) Elaeocarpus Ganitrus (b) Vinca rosea (c) Amyris Balsamifera (d) Phlogocanthus Thyrsiflorus

431. Which one of the following is the latest method of treating different cancers?
(a) Antibiotics (b) X-ray therapy (c) Nuclear medicine (d) Clinical medicine

432. Which of the following is a recent treatment for breast cancer?
(a) Isometrics (b) Hormone therapy (c) Thermotherapy (d) Cardiotherapy

433. Which one of the following proteins can be used in tumour therapy?
(a) Albumins (b) Keratin (c) Interferons (d) Glycoprotein

434. Which of the following is given to patients suffering from leukaemia?
(a) Transfusion of blood products (b) Glucose (c) Saline (d) Vitamin K injections

Cardiovascular drugs

435. Drugs that are useful in relaxing the blood vessels and thereby increasing the blood flow are known as:
(a) Sclerosing agents (b) Vasodilators (c) Vasoconstrictors (d) Vasopressin

436. Vasodilators are used in the treatment of:
(a) Aneurysms (b) Asthma (c) Angina pectoris (d) Varicose veins

437. One of the following drugs is a vasodilator. Which one is it?
(a) Dactinomycin (b) Griseofulvin (c) Penicillin (d) Glyceryl Trinitrate

438. What is a hypotensive drug?

(a) A drug that decreases blood pressure (b) A drug that increases blood pressure (c) A drug that constricts the heart (d) A drug that activates the heart

439. Which of the following is a hypotensive drug?

(a) Diazoxide (b) Antergan (c) Mepyramine (d) Haloperidol

440. Which of the following drugs reduces the high cholesterol level in serum?

(a) Mersalyl (b) Reserpine (c) Interferon (d) Clofibrate

441. Which of the following is an antiarrhythmic drug that was introduced in the early part of the twentieth century?

(a) Sulphaphenazole (b) Quinidine (c) Clotrimazole (d) Sulphadiazine

442. Certain people suffer from abnormal rhythm of the heart. What type of drugs are given to them?

(a) Cardio accelerators (b) Sedatives (c) Hypotensive drug (d) Antiarrhythmics

443. Some people suffer from a poor circulation of blood because of the heart pumping poorly. Which drugs are used to gear up the heart to pump properly?

(a) Cardiotonics (b) Antispasmodics (c) Anodynes (d) Cardiac Depressors

444. Which of the following drugs is a cardiotonic?

(a) Benzocaine (b) Digoxin (c) Ismelin (d) Oxyphenbutazone

445. Which of the following drugs brings down blood pressure?

(a) Beta-blocker (b) Cardiac glycosides (c) Sclerosing agents (d) Immuno-suppressive drugs

446. Which of the following drugs is a vasodilator?

(a) Digitalis (b) Reserpine (c) Methyl dopa (d) Cyclandelate

447. Which of the following drugs is a beta-blocker?

(a) Amyl nitrate (b) Metoprolol (c) Oubain
(d) Digitoxine
448. Which of the following categories of drugs lessens
the activity of the heart?
(a) Vasostimulants (b) Cardiotonics (c) Beta-block-
ers (d) Vasodilators

Diuretics
449. A drug that increases the amount of urine excreted
by the kidneys is known as:
(a) Antidiuretic (b) Diuretic (c) Cathartic (d) Anthelmintic
450. The treatment of which of the following is done
by diuretics?
(a) Oedema (b) Fever (c) Peptic ulcer (d) Diabetes
451. Which of the following drugs has a diuretic action?
(a) Digitalis (b) Clotrimazole (c) Cycloserine
(d) Cephalexin
452. Which of the following hormones is a powerful
antidiuretic?
(a) Progesterone (b) Aldosterone (c) Insulin
(d) Testosterone
453. Lasix is a commonly used diuretic. What is the
other name for it?
(a) Muscarine (b) Persantine (c) Furosemide
(d) Fusidic acid

Drugs used in tuberculosis
454. Which of the following characteristics must an
antitubercular drug have?
(a) Antiallergic (b) Antiviral (c) Respiratory
depressant (d) Bacteriostatic
455. Which of the following drugs is used in the
chemotherapy of tuberculosis?
(a) Papaverine (b) Isoniazid (c) Mannitol
(d) Chlorambucil

456. Ethambutol is a drug that is used in the treatment of tuberculosis. What is the other name for ethambutol?
(a) Myambutol (b) Crotamiton (c) Salbutamol (d) Ergocalciferol

457. Which of the following antitubercular drugs is obtained from streptomyces mediterrani?
(a) Dapsone (b) Cycloserine (c) Rifampin (d) Pyrazinamide

Drugs used for mental diseases

458. Drugs that are used on mental patients to bring their excitation and aggressiveness under control are known as:
(a) Tranquillizers (b) Carminatives (c) Decoction (d) Hallucinogens

459. A tranquillizer acts by lowering the activity of the:
(a) Central nervous system (b) Heart (c) Liver (d) Stomach

460. Which of the following drugs has been isolated from Rauwolfia serpentina and is useful for the treatment of schizophrenia?
(a) Pempidine (b) Reserpine (c) Hydralazine (d) Nifedipine

461. Which of the following drugs is used for the treatment of major psychic disorders like paranoia and schizophrenia?
(a) Atoxyl (b) Tolazoline (c) Trifluperidol (d) Frusemide

462. Which of the following drugs is used to relieve anxiety?
(a) Meprobamate (b) Antipyrine (c) Merbaphen (d) Ibuprofen

463. Which of the following drugs is used for inducing sleep?
(a) Benadryl (b) Diazepam (c) Amyl nitrite (d) Cytarabin

464. Which of the following drugs calms down a lunatic?
(a) Haloperidol (b) Homatropine (c) Theobromine (d) Diathiazamine

465. Certain drugs are employed to activate the nervous system. What are they categorized as?
(a) Barbiturates (b) Neuroleptics (c) Sedatives (d) Amphetamines

466. Hallucinogenic drugs disturb the brain and produce unnatural and abnormal thoughts and emotions. Which of the following is a hallucinogenic drug?
(a) Meprobamate (b) LSD (c) Trifluperidol (d) Thiothixene

467. Which of the following drugs activates the nervous system?
(a) Methotrexate (b) Tetracycline (c) Methedrine (d) Haloperidol

468. What is a drug that pacifies the nerves known as?
(a) A sedative (b) A neurotonic (c) A neurovaccine (d) An amphetamine

469. A drug that produces sleep is known as:
(a) Cardiac depressant (b) Hypnotic (c) Antihypnotic (d) Antihypertensive

470. Which of the following is a hypnotic drug?
(a) Caffeine (b) Barbiturate (c) Nardil (d) Doxepin

471. Which of the following acts like a sedative?
(a) Ergot alkaloids (b) Ibuprofen (c) Valium (d) Mephenesin

Miscellaneous
472. Which of the following is used to combat Kala-azar?
(a) Clofazimine (b) Tinidazole (c) Methyldopa (d) Pentamidine isethionate

473. Which of the following is useful in the treatment of baldness?
(a) Minoxidil (b) Bacitracin (c) Sulphacetamide (d) Ampicillin sodium

474. A cholagogue functions by activating the bile flow from the gall bladder. Which of the following drugs functions as a cholagogue?
(a) Carbenoxolone (b) Sodium taurocholate (c) Phenytoin (d) Prednisolone

475. To which of the following group of drugs does lysergic acid diethylamide (LSD) belong?
(a) Antianxiety drugs (b) Hallucinogens (c) Antipsychotics (d) Analgesics

476. With which of the following may early symptoms of peptic ulcer be treated?
(a) Antihistamines (b) Anti-amoebics (c) Antacids (d) Diuretics

477. How does an antacid function?
(a) By neutralizing the excess hydrochloric acid in the stomach (b) By decreasing acid secretion in the stomach (c) By increasing pepsin concentration in the stomach (d) By stopping acid secretion in the stomach

478. A drug that is used to prevent vomiting is known as:
(a) Antiemetic (b) Digestant (c) Antidote (d) Emetic

479. A scientist in Argentina has discovered that he can cure a particular skin disease by tattooing with gold salts. Which is this skin disease?
(a) Psoriasis (b) Leprosy (c) Leukoderma (d) Chilblain

480. Which of the following drugs is mostly used for curing duodenal ulcers?
(a) Analgin (b) Cimetidine (c) Paracetamol (d) Aspirin

481. Certain drugs are employed in transplant operations in order to prevent the body from rejecting

the transplanted organs. What are these drugs known as?
(a) Antimetabolites (b) Immunosuppressive drugs (c) Steroids (d) Hormones

482. Which of the following is an immunosuppressive drug?
(a) Cyclosporin (b) Caffeine (c) Loperamide (d) Ranitidine Hydrochloride

483. Which of the following drugs is used in the treatment of AIDS?
(a) Penicillin (b) Streptozocin (c) Diclofenac Sodium (d) Azidothymidine

484. Which of the following drugs can be administered in the case of malaria in which Chloroquine does not work?
(a) Cortisone (b) Mefloquine (c) Ibuprofen (d) Procaine

485. Which of the following works to reduce the effect of poison from a scorpion bite?
(a) Ammonia, lime water (b) Dettol (c) Water (d) Cold cream

486. What are drugs employed in the treatment of myasthenia gravis known as?
(a) Barbiturates (b) Antimyasthenics (c) Muscle relaxants (d) Sulphonamides

487. Drugs that are used to relax muscles and thus lessen the pain from muscle injury are known as:
(a) Antiarthritic (b) Vesicant (c) Prophylactic (d) Muscle relaxants

488. A new immunosuppressive agent was discovered in Japan in 1984. Which is it?
(a) AB 325 (b) FK 506 (c) CZ 931 (d) FG 501

489. The bacteria streptomyces tsukubaents produces:
(a) Streptomycin (b) Tetracycline (c) FK 506 (d) Penicillin

490. Researchers from which country have used FK 506 in liver and kidney transplant and reported their work in *Lancet*, the medical journal?

(a) USA (b) Indonesia (c) India (d) Thailand

491. From which of the following was the immuno-suppressive drug Cyclosporin isolated?
(a) Penicillium notatum (b) Tolypocladium inflatum (c) B. subtilis (d) Aspergillus flavus

492. Which of the following is effective against diarrhoea?
(a) Brazil root (b) Roots of Elaeocarpus ganitrus (c) Beet root (d) Roots of Vinca rosea

493. Which of the following brings relief to patients suffering from rheumatoid arthritis?
(a) Ultraviolet rays (b) X-rays (c) Acupuncture (d) Radiotherapy

494. Which of the following category of drugs is used in the treatment of psoriasis?
(a) Enzymes (b) Corticosteroids (c) Hormones (d) Antifungals

495. Which of the following agents is inactive and is administered only to appease the patient's desire for medicine?
(a) Placebo (b) Anabolic steroids (c) Sedatives (d) Narcotics

6

DISEASES CAUSED BY DRUGS

496. Studies show that prolonged use of corticosteroids for the eyes is harmful. Which of the following does it cause?
(a) Astigmatism (b) Glaucoma (c) Myopia (d) Hypermetropia

497. Mental retardation has been found to take place in a child born to a mother who has received:
(a) Pelvic X-ray (b) Pelvic ultrasonography (c) Infra-red rays (d) Fat rich diet

498. Chlorambucil is given to patients suffering from Hodgkin's disease. Which of the following

manifests itself in children born to mothers treated
with chlorambucil?

(a) Typhoid (b) Congenital malformations
(c) Jaundice (d) Rubella

499. Teratogenic effects have been found to be
associated with which of the following?

(a) Excessive intake of Vitamin B2 (b) Excessive
intake of Vitamin D (c) Excessive intake of Vitamin
E (d) Steroidal formulations

500. Which hypnotic drug was responsible for the birth
of several deformed children?

(a) Thalidomide (b) Cyclobarbitone (c) Phenobarbital (d) Valium

501. Which of the following symptoms is found in
babies born to mothers who are drug addicts?

(a) Stomach aches (b) Hypercalcaemia (c) Bleeding gums (d) Withdrawal effects

502. Babies suffer from stuffy nose and respiratory
trouble when born to mothers undergoing
treatment with:

(a) Iron (b) Vitamins (c) Hormones (d) Reserpine

503. Which of the following is sometimes found in
babies born to mothers undergoing treatment with
Chloramphenicol?

(a) Gray baby syndrome (b) Measles (c) Jaundice
(d) Syphilis

504. Antimalarials should be administered carefully and
in proper dosage since they harm:

(a) The ears (b) The nose (c) The eyes (d) The
brain

505. Oral thrush has been found to be associated with
which of the following?

(a) Analgesics (b) Antipyretics (c) Emetics
(d) Broad spectrum antibiotics

506. Patients should be tested for allergic symptoms
before receiving which of the following?

(a) Penicillin (b) Ampicillin (c) Amoxycillin
(d) Trimethoprin

507. Laxatives should not be used regularly for they may lead to:
(a) Diarrhoea (b) Chronic constipation (c) Nausea (d) Anorexia

508. Nose drops should not be used often and randomly for it may give the effect of a permanent nose-block by:
(a) Overexpansion of the blood vessels in the nasal tract (b) Increasing the number of hair present in the nasal tract (c) Increasing the chances of catching cold (d) Decreasing resistance

509. Children suffering from influenza or chicken pox and undergoing treatment with aspirin have in many cases been the victims of a disease called:
(a) Down's syndrome (b) Fragile-X syndrome (c) Reye's syndrome (d) Epilepsy

510. A drug that has been found to interfere with the making of the protective mucous lining of the stomach wall and thereby causing ulcer is:
(a) Analgin (b) Aspirin (c) Paracetamol (d) Both (a) and (c)

511. Patients suffering from peptic ulcer show worsening of the disease if they have resorted to a particular painkiller for lessening the pain. Which is this painkiller?
(a) Paracetamol (b) Aspirin (c) Analgin (d) None

512. The drug Paramethadione has been found to produce abnormal and defective children in mothers undergoing treatment with this. For the treatment of which disease is this drug used?
(a) Epilepsy (b) Leukaemia (c) Glioma (d) Gastric ulcer

513. Expectant mothers should abstain from alcohol, for they may give birth to babies suffering from:
(a) Reye's syndrome (b) Foetal alcohol syndrome (c) Gray baby syndrome (d) Down's syndrome

514. Foetal abnormalities have been found to occur in expectant mothers receiving:

(a) Anticancer drugs (b) Antiemetics (c) Vitamin K injection (d) Laxatives

515. Which of the following is exhibited by offsprings born to expectant mothers treated with Tetracyclines?
(a) Small teeth (b) Large teeth (c) Yellow teeth (d) Pure white teeth

516. Symptoms of jaundice and pyridoxine deficiency have been found to occur in patients undergoing treatment with Isoniazid. Which disease are they suffering from?
(a) Rhinitis (b) Tuberculosis (c) Colitis (d) Gastric ulcer

517. Deep X-ray therapy which was used for the treatment of spondylitis is in less use now. Why is it so?
(a) Fear of causing osteoporosis (b) Fear of causing leukaemia (c) Fear of causing migraine (d) Fear of causing arthritis

518. Which of the following has been found to cause liver damage?
(a) Novalgin (b) Diazepam (c) Propanolol (d) Pyrazinamide

519. Ulceration of the mouth and lips has been found to occur with an anticancer drug. Which one is it?
(a) Cisplatin (b) Chlorambucil (c) Cyclophosphamide (d) Mitomycin-C

520. Antacids based on aluminium should not be used for long, as they may lead to:
(a) Cardiac arrest (b) Hypertension (c) Glioma (d) Softening of the bones

521. Which of the following is caused by many oral contraceptives?
(a) Weight gain (b) Weight loss (c) Arthritis (d) Insomnia

522. Which of the following has been found to cause liver damage?

71

(a) Aspirin (b) Cholecalciferol (c) Salicylamide
(d) Methotrexate
523. Ultra-violet rays have been found useful in the treatment of psoriasis. However, excessive use of ultra-violet rays has been found to cause:
(a) Dermatitis (b) Rheumatism (c) Skin cancer
(d) Xeroderma
524. Which of the following is a result of prolonged use of Chloramphenicol?
(a) Anaemia (b) Dentalgia (c) Tyrosinosis (d) Cystinuria
525. Tetracycline should not be administered to which of the following?
(a) Young mothers (b) Middle-aged mothers
(c) Old people (d) Teenagers
526. Baldness is associated with many anticancer drugs. Which of the following antibiotic causes baldness?
(a) Penicillin (b) Ampicillin (c) Dactinomycin
(d) Amoxycillin

7
DIAGNOSTIC TESTS AND TOOLS

Tests
527. Which of the following tests is used to detect AIDS?
(a) ELISA test (b) Rubin test (c) Wassermann test
(d) Patch test
528. Which of the following tests is used to detect anaemia?
(a) Test for blood urea (b) Blood typing
(c) Haemoglobin in blood test (d) Babcock's test
529. Which of the following tests is used to detect malaria?
(a) Urine test (b) X-ray examination (c) Blood test
(d) Jolles's test

530. Which of the following tests is used to detect typhoid?
(a) Hirschberg's test (b) Johnson's test (c) Sackett's test (d) Widal's test

531. Which of the following tests is used to detect diabetes mellitus?
(a) Checking bilirubin in blood (b) Checking albumin in urine (c) Checking blood sugar level (d) Checking haemoglobin level in blood

532. To determine which of the following is Sackett's method used?
(a) Calcium in blood (b) Cholesterol in blood (c) Haemoglobin in blood (d) RBCs in blood

533. To detect lesions of the alimentary canal the faeces are tested for:
(a) Worms (b) Giardiasis (c) Occult blood (d) Mucous

534. The level of bilirubin in blood is measured to detect jaundice. Which test does this?
(a) Dynamography (b) Van den Bergh's test (c) Millon's test (d) Millard's test

535. To study chronic liver disease tests are carried out to determine:
(a) Urea in blood (b) Serum bilirubin (c) Level of hydrochloric acid in the stomach (d) Blood count

536. Which is the confirmatory test for AIDS?
(a) Western blot test (b) Wool test (c) Chrobak test (d) Acetone test

537. What is the ELISA test acronym for?
(a) Enzyme-linked immunodeficiency assay (b) Enzyme-linked immunosorbent assay (c) Enzyme-linked sorbic acid assay (d) Enzyme-linked immuno deficiency syndrome assay

538. A particular type of blood test can detect syphilis in a patient. Which test is this?
(a) Widal test (b) Wassermann test (c) Blood urea test (d) Differential blood count

539. Which of the following tests is carried out to detect worm infestation?
(a) Blood test (b) Stool examination (c) Urine test (d) X-ray

540. Which test is used to indicate the presence of albumin in urine?
(a) Allen-Doisy test (b) Biuret test (c) Rubin test (d) Millard's test

Instruments

541. A machine that keeps up blood circulation while the heart is stopped during surgery is known as:
(a) Pacemaker (b) Heart-lung machine (c) Angioscope (d) Electrocardiograph

542. An instrument that is used to monitor the development of an unborn baby is known as:
(a) Ultrasonic equipment (b) Horismascope (c) Hemoxometer (d) Intensimeter

543. What is the full name of CAT scanner?
(a) Computerized antitomographic scanner
(b) Computerized angular tomographic scanner
(c) Computerized axial tomographic scanner
(d) Computerized axial topical scanner

544. By which of the following can cerebral haemorrhage be detected?
(a) CAT scanner (b) Blood test (c) Barium X-ray (d) Ultrasonography

545. By which of the following are electrical changes in the brain studied?
(a) Dielectrolysis (b) Electroencephalograph (c) Kahn's test (d) Drechsel's test

546. By which of the following instruments can heart disorders be detected?
(a) Radiograph (b) Potentiograph (c) Thermograph (d) Electrocardiograph

547. The gastrointestinal tract is made visible on the X-ray plate by the use of a certain chemical compound. Which diagnostic tool is it?

(a) Skiagraphy (b) Barium X-ray (c) NMR (d) Ultrasonography

548. Which instrument is used to hear the sound of the heart and lungs?
(a) Duane's clinometer (b) Cardioscope (c) Enterotome (d) Stethoscope

549. Which of the following is used to examine the eyes?
(a) Ophthalmoscope (b) X-ray (c) Epidiascope (d) Photo-electron microscope

550. An instrument that is used to check the ears is known as:
(a) Acouphone (b) Otoscope (c) Acousticon (d) Otophone

551. By which of the following can disturbances in the retina of the eye be detected?
(a) Iridology (b) Electroretinography (c) Skiagraphy (d) Lymphography

552. The quantification of oxygen present in the blood can be done by an instrument known as:
(a) Hemoxometer (b) Sphygmometer (c) Skiameter (d) Litrameter

553. Which one of the following is a diagnostic tool used to detect aneurysms, by injecting an iodine compound and then studying by X-rays?
(a) Lumbar puncture (b) Chromoscopy (c) Sonography (d) Angiography

554. Apart from X-rays the latest machine that is used to take images of the internal parts of the body is known as:
(a) Electron microscope (b) Metabolimeter (c) Oxinhalator (d) NMR imaging machine

555. What is the advantage of resorting to NMR imaging over X-ray imaging?
(a) Less expensive (b) More easily available (c) Does not harm the body (d) Less time consuming

556. An instrument that measures the radiation exposure that a person has gone through is known as:
(a) Dynamometer (b) Energometer (c) Glycosometer (d) Dosimeter

557. Diseases of the bones and organs are studied with the help of:
(a) Gas chromatography (b) Radiology (c) Liquid Chromatography (d) Thermograph

558. By which of the following are diseases of the nervous system studied?
(a) Spirometry (b) Rothera's test (c) Neuroradiology (d) Koroscopy

559. A patient is administered anaesthesia and a surgical telescope is inserted into her abdominal cavity to check for blocked fallopian tubes. Which is this diagnostic tool?
(a) Vasectomy (b) Laparoscopy (c) Lobotomy (d) Endoscopy

560. What is hysterosalpinogram?
(a) It is a special type of X-ray that is used to detect blocked fallopian tubes (b) It is a surgical operation by which the uterus is removed (c) It is a surgical operation by which the ovaries are removed (d) It is used to remove cancerous cells

561. Why do dental X-rays have less ionising radiation hazards compared to X-rays of other parts of the body?
(a) Because the instrument functions at a high voltage (b) Because the instrument functions at a relatively low voltage (c) Because the instrument is battery operated (d) Because the X-rays emitted lack ionizing power

562. Sometimes ordinary X-rays do not give a clear picture of tumours in the jaws or fractures of the joint bones, etc. Which form of diagnosis is then resorted to?

(a) Tomography (b) Ultrasonography (c) Angiography (d) Rheotachygraphy

563. When the entire jaw area is studied with the help of tomography, the resulting film is known as:
(a) Radiogram (b) Panagram (c) Tachogram (d) Encephalogram

564. To study and detect abnormal changes in shape, hardness or softness of parts of the body an instrument is used. What is its name?
(a) Myelotome (b) Percussion hammer (c) Pleximeter (d) Percussion stethoscope

565. Deafness is diagnosed with the help of a tuning fork. Which test is this?
(a) Widal test (b) Wool test (c) Babcock's test (d) Weber's test

566. The refractive errors of the eye are studied with the help of:
(a) Iridectome (b) Ophthalmostat (c) Retinoscope (d) Ophthalmometer

567. Which of the following types of diagnoses is resorted to in orthodontics?
(a) Organoscopy (b) Cholangiography (c) NMR (d) Cephalometric radiography

568. An instrument that is useful in the study of the cerebral cavities is known as:
(a) Teleradiography (b) Ventriculoscope (c) Cephalemometer (d) Cephalometer

569. A common instrument that is used by doctors to measure arterial blood pressure is known as:
(a) Sphygmomanometer (b) Sphymometer (c) Sphygmophone (d) Sphygmochronograph

570. Which is the latest diagnostic tool that finds the exact location of coronary diseases and tells the extent of the damage?
(a) Electron microscope (b) Cardiopneumograph (c) Cardiotachometer (d) Thallium scintillography

571. Which of the following is used to diagnose disorders of the muscles?

77

(a) Tachography (b) Electromyography (c) Rheo-tachygraphy (d) Myelography

572. The method of passing a flexible telescope through the anus to study the bowels is known as:
(a) Laparoscopy (b) Endoscopy (c) Colonoscopy (d) Peritoneoscopy

573. For which type of patients is peritoneoscopy helpful?
(a) Patients with gastric ulcer (b) Patients with ascites (c) Patients with colitis (d) Patients with duodenal ulcer

574. Which of the following is used to tell how much glucose is present in a sample of urine?
(a) Cardiograph (b) Dioptometer (c) Diabeto-meter (d) Potentiograph

575. Which instrument helps in viewing the inside of the stomach?
(a) Rectoscope (b) Gastroscope (c) Keratometer (d) Lithotriptoscope

576. Which is the mode of diagnosis that is resorted to in epilepsy?
(a) X-ray (b) ECG (c) Electroencephalography (d) Blood test

577. Injuries of the nervous system are detected with the help of:
(a) Immunoassays (b) Monoclonal antibodies (c) Cytology (d) Neuroradiology

578. To study defects in the kidneys which of the following X-ray techniques is used?
(a) Barium X-ray (b) Pyelography (c) Mammo-graphy (d) Skiagraphy

579. Which one of the following instruments is used to measure the extent of deafness?
(a) Keratometer (b) Otophone (c) Diplopiometer (d) Audiometer

580. What is the other name for X-rays derived from the name of its discoverer?

(a) Roentgen rays (b) Cosmic rays (c) α-rays (d) Radioactive rays

581. In order to measure the rate at which blood is flowing, which of the following is resorted to?
(a) Oariotomy (b) Tachography (c) Echoencephalography (d) Radionuclide imaging

582. Which one of the following methods can be resorted to in order to detect tumours of the spinal cord?
(a) Verne's test (b) Chrobak test (c) Gelle's test (d) Myelography

Miscellaneous

583. In which of the following diseases is lumber puncture resorted to?
(a) Meningitis (b) Slip disc (c) Spondylitis (d) Osteoarthritis

584. The microscopic examination of a part of the tissue removed from a cancerous growth is known as:
(a) Iridotomy (b) Jolles's test (c) Biopsy (d) Endoscopy

585. To identify a person and his parentage the state of the art diagnostic tool is:
(a) RNA fingerprinting (b) DNA fingerprinting (c) Embryology (d) Lithology

586. The contents of the stomach are taken out by a tube inserted from the mouth to study:
(a) The level of gastric juice (b) The level of food digested (c) The level of food intake (d) The level of water intake

587. A high level of hydrochloric acid and blood are present in the stomach contents of patients suffering from:
(a) Cholera (b) Colitis (c) Peritonitis (d) Gastric ulcer

588. Cytogenetics is used to study:

(a) Protein metabolism (b) Chromosomal abnormality (c) Vitamin B deficiency (d) Vitamin A deficiency

589. Which of the following tests is used to detect mental retardation?
(a) Enzyme analysis (b) Chromosomal analysis (c) Amino acid analysis (d) Bone analysis

590. Which one of the following tests helps diagnose mental diseases?
(a) Rinne test (b) Szabo's test (c) Acetone test (d) Rorschach test

591. People suffering from colour blindness may have to undergo one of the following tests. Which one is that?
(a) Widal test (b) Wool test (c) Szabo's test (d) Babcock's test

592. A test that may be carried out for the detection of the typhus group of fevers is known as:
(a) Rorschach test (b) Weil-Felix test (c) Chrobak test (d) Gelle's test

593. One of the latest diagnostic kits in India has been developed by the National Institute of Immunology, Delhi, to detect the HCG hormone. Which diagnosis will this kit help?
(a) Pregnancy and cancer (b) Heart attack (c) Kidney failure (d) Glioma

594. The test employed to distinguish between gram-positive and gram-negative microorganisms is known as:
(a) Lieben's test (b) Biuret test (c) Gram stain (d) Schiller's test

595. X-ray examination, Mantoux's test, and sputum culture are done for the diagnosis of:
(a) Cancer (b) Tuberculosis (c) Malaria (d) Filaria

596. The diagnosis of which of the following diseases is resorted to by fiberoptic transbronchial lung biopsy?

(a) Pulmonary tuberculosis (b) Pneumonia (c) Meningitis (d) Miliary tuberculosis

597. Which test is utilised for the diagnosis of syphilis?
(a) Rubin test (b) Dowell test (c) Kahn test (d) Acetone test

598. The latest technique of performing biopsy by a syringe and a fine needle is known as:
(a) FNAB technique (b) FWAB technique (c) FQRS technique (d) FOAB technique

599. Which of the following is employed in liver scanning to detect diseases of the liver?
(a) Proteins (b) Radioactive isotopes (c) Enzymes (d) Hormones

600. Which of the following diagnoses is carried out in Hodgkin's disease?
(a) Lymphnode biopsy (b) ECG (c) Stool examination (d) Urine culture

601. In which test is the ammiotic fluid tested during pregnancy to detect defects in the foetus?
(a) Ultrasonography (b) Wool test (c) Amniocentesis (d) Rinne test

602. The fractional Test Meal technique is used in the diagnosis of:
(a) Jaundice (b) Acidity (c) Nausea (d) Loss of appetite

603. Which of the following is used in cancer diagnosis?
(a) Nephelometry (b) Turbidimetry (c) Angiography (d) Flow cytometry

604. Which of the following will become a very powerful diagnostic tool against various cancers in the near future?
(a) Monoclonal antibodies (b) Electrophoresis (c) X-rays (d) Cobalt rays

605. Monoclonal antibodies are produced by a tissue culture technique. What is the name of this technique?
(a) Fermentation (b) Hybridoma technique (c) Biopsy (d) Tissue extract

606. Nowadays early detection of certain carcinomas is possible with the help of:
(a) Radioimmunoassay (b) X-rays (c) Ultrasonography (d) Colourimetry

8
NUTRITION AND DIET

Nutrients

607. Carbohydrates, proteins, minerals, fats, and vitamins are required by the body for growth, for deriving energy, etc. What are these known as?
(a) Nutriants (b) Nutrients (c) Nutrin (d) Nutrabin

608. How does intake of carrots prevent Vitamin A deficiency?
(a) Carrots contain carotenoids which are converted to Vitamin A in the body (b) Carrots contain Vitamin A (c) Carrots contain certain enzymes which help in the synthesis of Vitamin A (d) Vitamin A present in carrots can be easily absorbed by the body

609. What is the other name for Vitamin B_1?
(a) Riboflavin (b) Thiamin (c) Pyridoxine (d) Ascorbic acid

610. A fat-free, low-protein diet may moderately reduce:
(a) Leukoderma (b) Dermatitis (c) Psoriasis (d) Eczema

611. The starches and sugars present in food come under the category of:
(a) Proteins (b) Amino acids (c) Carbohydrates (d) Enzymes

612. Carbohydrates are metabolised in the body to produce:
(a) Vitamins (b) Blood (c) Muscles (d) Energy

613. Food containing this produces good development of bones and a healthy skin:
(a) Vitamin A (b) Sugar (c) Salt (d) Vitamin K

614. What is the other name for Vitamin B2?
(a) Thiamin (b) Riboflavin (c) Pyridoxine (d) Niacin

615. Which of the following is needed by the body to utilize sugars and starches?
(a) Vitamin B12 (b) Sodium (c) Iodine (d) Thiamin

616. What is Vitamin B12 also known as?
(a) Cyanocobalamin (b) Niacin (c) Riboflavin (d) Pyridoxine

617. What is pyridoxine commonly referred to as?
(a) Vitamin B1 (b) Vitamin B2 (c) Vitamin B12 (d) Vitamin B6

618. The body requires Vitamin B12 and folic acid to make:
(a) Skin (b) Red blood cells (c) Teeth (d) Bones

619. Lactose is present in milk. To which category does it belong?
(a) Proteins (b) Carbohydrates (c) Vitamins (d) Amino acids

620. Calcium, phosphorus, potassium, sulphur, sodium, etc., are present in milk. What are these substances known as?
(a) Nutrose (b) Proteins (c) Minerals (d) Enzymes

621. Which of the following is the protein matter in milk?
(a) Casein (b) Keratin (c) Protamin (d) Gluten

622. Modern research has shown that free radicals, which are short-lived chemical fragments, are generated during metabolism in the body. These cause damage to the body tissues and hence cause ageing. Which one of the following elements in our diet can change the free radicals into less harmful substances?

(a) Sodium (b) Potassium (c) Selenium (d) Copper

623. An element which is now considered to be essential in our diet and which is named after the moon goddess has been found to have anticarcinogenic properties. Which one of the following is it?
(a) Selenium (b) Calcium (c) Iron (d) Zinc

624. What is the function of proteins in the body?
(a) To build bones (b) To build tissues (c) To help digestion (d) To give sexual energy

625. In what way do carbohydrates and fats help the body?
(a) They provide heat and energy (b) They maintain the body temperature (c) They prevent viral diseases (d) They give protection against fungal diseases

626. A vitamin that is essential for bone formation exists in two forms known as cholecalciferol and ergocalciferol. Which is this vitamin?
(a) Vitamin A (b) Vitamin C (c) Vitamin D (d) Vitamin E

627. Why does Vitamin D and calcium go hand in hand for the growth of bones?
(a) Because calcium and Vitamin D are converted into bones in the stomach (b) Because calcium and Vitamin D combine together to form bones in the pancreas (c) Calcium helps in the absorption of Vitamin D in the body (d) Bones require enough calcium for growing and Vitamin D helps in the absorption of calcium from the intestine

628. A particular nutrient is required by the body for haemoglobin synthesis. It is found in liver, meat, spinach, etc. Which one is it?
(a) Chromium (b) Calcium (c) Iron (d) Magnesium

629. In order to satisfy the nutritional requirements of the body, a person who consumes alcohol should

take adequate doses of a certain group of vitamins. Which of the following is that group?

(a) Vitamins A and E (b) Vitamins K and D (c) Vitamins of the B group (d) Vitamins A and B

630. What type of a diet should be given to a person who has sustained burn injuries?

(a) Diet devoid of B group of vitamins (b) Diet devoid of Vitamin C (c) Diet rich in Vitamin E (d) Vitamins and protein-rich diet

631. Water used for boiling vegetables should not be thrown away since this will involve rejecting a particular essential vitamin which this water contains. Which is this vitamin?

(a) Vitamin K (b) Vitamin D (c) Vitamin E (d) Thiamin

632. Which of the following nutrients are lost, if rice is washed for long before cooking?

(a) Proteins (b) Vitamin A (c) Vitamin E (d) B group of vitamins

633. Parboiled rice is considered more nutritive compared to polished raw rice. Which nutrient does it have in greater quantity?

(a) Magnesium (b) Thiamin (c) Calcium (d) Vitamin B_{12}

Sources

634. Which of the following are good sources of Vitamin B_1?

(a) Beer (b) White of egg (c) Wine, lemon juice (d) Pork, wheat, fresh vegetables

635. Vitamin E is available in:

(a) Fish (b) Pork (c) Vegetable oils (d) Beef

636. Among the food we eat which of the following is a common source of starch?

(a) Carrots (b) Tomatoes (c) Apples (d) Bread

637. Fish liver, and yellow and green vegetables are a good source of:

(a) Iodine (b) Fluorine (c) Sodium (d) Vitamin A

638. Meat, wheat, fresh vegetables, peas, beans, etc., are rich in:
(a) Vitamin B_1 (b) Vitamin L (c) Chromium (d) Fluorine

639. Vegetables, milk, and liver are rich in:
(a) Iodine (b) Vitamin B_2 (c) Sodium (d) Linoleic acid

640. Liver is a rich source of:
(a) Vitamin D (b) Vitamin E (c) Vitamin B_{12} (d) Cobalt

641. Green and leafy vegetables are a rich source of:
(a) Folic acid (b) Cobalt (c) Both (a) and (b) (d) Iodine

642. Which of the following is an excellent source of Vitamins A and C?
(a) Mango (b) Wheat (c) Potatoes (d) Rice

643. Sodium is required by the body to maintain the pH of blood apart from other functions. Which of the following is rich in sodium?
(a) Tomatoes (b) Cheese (c) Potatoes (d) Bananas

644. Which of the following food items provides a rich source of calcium?
(a) Citrus fruits (b) Dried yeast (c) Milk (d) Vegetable oil

645. Magnesium is a nutrient that is required by the body to make teeth and bones. Which of the following has magnesium in it?
(a) Milk (b) Carrots (c) Nuts (d) Salt

646. Tomatoes are a rich source of:
(a) Chromium (b) Vitamin C (c) Iodine (d) Copper

647. The body requires phosphorus to make bones and teeth. Which of the following is a source of phosphorus?
(a) Fish (b) Meat (c) Yeast (d) Both (a) and (b)

648. The yolk of an egg contains a particular vitamin belonging to the B group. Which is this vitamin?

(a) Riboflavin (b) Pyridoxine (c) Biotin (d) Niacin

649. Jaggery is recommended for anaemic patients. What is the reason for this?
(a) It is rich in iron (b) It is rich in chromium (c) It is rich in phosphorus (d) It is rich in magnesium

650. Apart from Vitamin C, mango and papaya contain:
(a) Linoleic acid (b) Magnesium (c) Carotene (d) Chromium

651. Proteins are present in sufficient quantity in:
(a) Tomatoes (b) Pulses (c) Pineapple (d) Bitter gourd

652. Spinach is a rich source of:
(a) Iron (b) Proteins (c) Fats (d) Carbohydrates

Deficiency diseases

653. What is the name of the disease in man arising out of Vitamin B_1 deficiency?
(a) Beriberi (b) Scurvy (c) Pellagra (d) Gingivitis

654. The deficiency of which of the following group of nutrients affects the skin?
(a) Iron, iodine, zinc, potassium (b) Riboflavin, niacin, pyridoxine, pantothenic acid (c) Vitamin K, calcium, fluorine, copper (d) All the three

655. What does niacin deficiency cause?
(a) Pellagra (b) Scurvy (c) Boils (d) Acne

656. What are the effects of Vitamin B_6 deficiency?
(a) Beriberi (b) Scurvy (c) Dermatomyoma (d) Certain types of eczema

657. Which of the following diseases is associated with Vitamin C deficiency?
(a) Psoriasis (b) Scurvy (c) Pellagra (d) Vitiligo

658. What does Vitamin K deficiency lead to?
(a) Problems in digestion (b) Problems in blood coagulation (c) Problems in calcium metabolism (d) All the three

659. Using purgatives on a regular basis is harmful to health. Which deficiency does it cause?

(a) Iron (b) Potassium (c) Iodine (d) Chromium

660. Deficiency of Vitamin D gives rise to:
(a) Rheumatism (b) Arthritis (c) Hernia (d) Rickets

661. What is the condition known as, in which the body does not get its fair share of nutrients, either from starvation, or as a result of poor absorption?
(a) Malnutrition (b) Marasmus (c) Kwashiorkor (d) Both (a) and (b)

662. Nightblindness, drying of the conjunctiva, dry and scaly skin and loss of hair are some of the symptoms of:
(a) Vitamin K deficiency (b) Vitamin A deficiency (c) Iron deficiency (d) Folic acid deficiency

663. Glycoprotein synthesis in the intestine is hindered due to the deficiency of:
(a) Iron (b) Selenium (c) Vitamin A (d) Copper

664. The deficiency of which of the following leads to stomatitis and magenta tongue?
(a) Vitamin K (b) Iron (c) Vitamin D (d) Vitamin B_2

665. Deficiency of iron in the body causes:
(a) Gingivitis (b) Anaemia (c) Glaucoma (d) Haemorrhage

666. Deficiency of magnesium causes:
(a) Growth retardation (b) Scurvy (c) Beriberi (d) Psoriasis

667. The deficiency of which of the following is seen in people who mainly eat polished rice?
(a) Vitamin B_1 (b) Vitamin K (c) Vitamin T (d) Iron

668. Anaemia and blood disorders are associated with the deficiency of:
(a) Thiamin (b) Riboflavin (c) Vitamin D (d) Vitamin B_{12} and folic acid

669. Which one of the following diseases results from protein deficiency?

(a) Huntington's disease (b) Pellagra
(c) Kwashiorkor (d) Diabetes mellitus

670. An expectant mother should have a balanced and proper diet, since malnutrition will increase the chances of:
(a) A deformed baby (b) A dull baby (c) A small baby (d) A baby with Down's syndrome

671. An expectant mother must take food which has an adequate supply of Vitamin D in order to avoid a bone disease known as:
(a) Rickets (b) Arthritis (c) Osteosarcoma (d) Osteomalacia

672. One must take iodized salt in one's diet in order to avoid iodine deficiency. Which disease occurs from iodine deficiency?
(a) Mongolism (b) Rubella (c) Goitre (d) Pellagra

Miscellaneous

673. The body cannot convert carotenes into Vitamin A very fast and hence excessive carotene intake causes:
(a) A yellow discoloration of the skin (b) Jaundice (c) Excess secretion of bile (d) A brown discoloration of the skin

674. Which of the following brings sparkle to the eyes when kept over the eyelids for some time?
(a) Used tea leaves (b) Used bay leaves (c) Used neem leaves (d) Used henna leaves

675. Which of the following has been found to improve glucose tolerance?
(a) Spinach (b) Brewer's yeast (c) Beetroot (d) Potatoes

676. The science that studies different aspects of foods and how the body utilizes them is known as:
(a) Dietotherapy (b) Nutrition (c) Science of metabolism (d) Science of condiments

677. The unit used to measure the energy provided by food is known as:

(a) Curie (b) Calorie (c) Joule (d) Watt

678. Vomiting, insomnia, night sweats, restlessness, etc., are the results of excessive dosage of:
(a) Vitamin A (b) Vegetables (c) Fruits (d) Vitamin B_1

679. Milk has a tinge of golden hue. What is it due to?
(a) Lactose (b) Casein (c) Fat (d) Carotene

680. The human body contains an enzyme that breaks down milk sugar. What is it?
(a) Protease (b) Lactase (c) Lipase (d) Amylase

681. Animal tissues have a substance called cholesterol which is fatty in nature. Patients with a high cholesterol level are advised to take:
(a) Whole milk (b) Butter (c) Skim milk (d) Hydrogenated fats

682. Many people cook potatoes after peeling off the skin. Which of the following vitamins are lost by discarding the peels?
(a) Vitamin P and Vitamin C (b) Vitamin K and Vitamin A (c) Vitamin B_1 and Vitamin B_2 (d) Vitamin B_6 and Niacin

683. It is good to eat pineapples after a diet of egg, meat, or fish. Why?
(a) Pineapples have cane sugar which helps protein metabolism (b) Pineapples have tartaric acid which reduces flatulence (c) It reduces insomnia (d) Bromelin, an enzyme present in pineapple, helps in the digestion of proteins

684. Nowadays, for lack of time, the urban population buys vegetables in bulk and freezes them and stores them. What happens to the nutritive value of such food?
(a) Remains the same (b) Decreases (c) Increases (d) The mineral content decreases

685. Chocolates are so tasty! The more one eats them, the more one wants. Why is it so?

(a) Because they are sweet, so one would like to eat more (b) Because they have a sophisticated bitter-sweet taste (c) Because chocolates contain theobromine which causes some addiction (d) Because chocolates contain theophylline which causes addiction

686. It has been observed that smoking brings down the level of Vitamin C in the body. Smokers should therefore make up for this deficiency by eating:
(a) Citrus fruits (b) Butter (c) Fish (d) Meat

687. Why does bread taste sweet when chewed for a long time?
(a) Because bread contains sugar (b) Because saliva contains sugar (c) Because saliva in the mouth changes starch in the bread into sugar (d) Because the taste buds secrete sugar

688. Why should food not be overcooked?
(a) Because overcooking makes the food tasteless (b) Because excessive heat destroys some nutritional properties of food (c) Because overcooking makes the food difficult to digest (d) Because overcooking makes the food toxic

689. People suffering from dyspepsia feel uncomfortable after eating food. The juice of a certain fruit taken after food gives relief. Which is this fruit?
(a) Apple (b) Pineapple (c) Bananas (d) Plums

690. The calorie requirement of the body increases in winter compared to summer. What is the reason for this?
(a) More calories are needed to sustain the temperature of the body (b) More calories are needed to make more fat in the body (c) More calories are needed to compensate for falling hair (d) More calories are needed to avoid the wasting of bones

691. Alcohol consumption increases in winter as against summer. Why?

(a) Alcohol makes the proteins more digestible
(b) The calorie content in alcohol is more, therefore the body temperature is maintained
(c) Alcohol helps in the digestion of vegetables
(d) One gets less drunk in winter than in summer

692. How does eating cooked egg help our body?
(a) Cooking an egg destroys avidin and thus helps the body to utilize biotin (b) Cooking an egg turns the albumin in the egg-white into pure protein (c) While cooking calcium from the shell enters the yolk and increases its calcium content (d) Cooking an egg makes it more nutritious

693. When food is boiled or cooked in water, Vitamin A is not destroyed. Why is it so?
(a) Vitamin A forms a complex with water (b) The stability of Vitamin A increases in boiling water (c) Vitamin A combines with the other vitamins and forms a complex (d) Vitamin A is an oil soluble vitamin, and therefore, does not dissolve out of the food in boiling water

694. How does cooking help in the digestion of food-grains?
(a) Cooking destroys the proteins thereby making the food easily digestible (b) Cooking breaks up the fibre content of food, thereby making the food easily digestible (c) Cooking makes the nutrients and starch easily available for digestion (d) Cooking breaks down the vitamins, thereby making digestion easy

695. Which of the following do sugar and jaggery mainly supply to the body?
(a) Thinking power (b) Energy (c) Sleep (d) Relaxation

696. In which of the following diseases is Vitamin B_{12} not absorbed from the intestine?
(a) Filaria (b) Rubella (c) Pernicious anaemia (d) Measles

697. A substance present in egg-white deactivates biotin, a B group vitamin. What is it?
(a) Avidin (b) Albumin (c) Sodium (d) Sulphur

698. Which of the following cures constipation and acts like a laxative?
(a) Sugar (b) Grapes (c) Starchy food (d) Iron capsules

699. Which one of the following is present in grapes in large amounts?
(a) Cellulose (b) Starch (c) Glucose (d) Salt

700. Grapes contain potassium salts and water. This makes them:
(a) A good diuretic (b) A bad diuretic (c) An antiemetic (d) An analgesic

701. Intake of which of the following helps maintain youth?
(a) Turmeric powder (b) Ginseng powder (c) Amla powder (d) Cardamom powder

702. Eating raw vegetables and diets with roughage helps in the natural cleansing of:
(a) Tooth surfaces (b) Body surfaces (c) Hair surfaces (d) Nail surfaces

703. Which one of the following elements is present in banana peels?
(a) Sodium (b) Potassium (c) Iodine (d) Iron

704. Mouldy groundnuts should not be eaten, for they may be contaminated by one of the following:
(a) Aspergillus fumigatus (b) Aspergillus flavus (c) Aspergillus glaucus (d) Penicillium glaucum

705. Which of the following diseases may occur on eating food contaminated by Aspergillus flavus?
(a) Migraine (b) Typhoid (c) Mumps (d) Liver cancer

706. Excessive consumption of smoked food is not good for health. Why?
(a) It may cause cancer of the stomach (b) It may cause cervical cancer (c) It may cause oral cancer (d) It may cause glioma

707. Frozen meat should be thawed properly and then cooked well to destroy the bacterium causing food poisoning. Which of the following is it?
(a) Candida albicans (b) B. subtilis (c) Salmonella (d) Mycobacterium leprae

708. Which of the following are found in pork?
(a) Thread worms (b) Round worms and tape worms (c) Whip worm (d) Ginuea worm

709. Which of the following should be taken by people living in very hot regions?
(a) Sufficient sugar (b) Excess vitamins (c) Sufficient salt and water (d) Excess proteins

710. Which of the following types of meal should be eaten by a diabetic person?
(a) Meals with high carbohydrate content (b) Meals with low carbohydrate content (c) Meals with low protein content (d) Meals with low vitamin content

711. Which chemical substance is responsible for the green colour in leafy vegetables?
(a) Iron (b) Sugar (c) Glycogen (d) Chlorophyll

712. When we cook green vegetables, why do they change colour?
(a) Because chlorophyll changes its colour on cooking (b) Because the vitamins change colour (c) Because iron changes colour (d) Because cellulose changes colour

713. Doctors often prescribe cod or shark liver oil for children. Why?
(a) Because it has iron (b) Because it has sodium (c) Because it has Vitamin C (d) Because it has Vitamins A and D

714. Eating food with more fibre content and drinking plenty of water is ideal for maintaining:
(a) A healthy heart (b) Healthy lungs (c) Healthy mind (d) A healthy bowel habit

9
SCIENTISTS AND DISCOVERIES

Anatomy

715. Who discovered the hormone insulin required to treat diabetes?
(a) Frederick Banting (b) Robert Koch (c) Gerhard Domagk (d) Alexander Fleming

716. Who isolated the hormone adrenalin in 1898?
(a) Albert B. Sabin (b) John J. Abel (c) Chain and Florey (d) Sir Julian Huxley

717. Who discovered the circulation of blood?
(a) Christian Barnard (b) William Harvey (c) Joseph Goldberger (d) Pythagoras

718. The existence of four blood groups A, B, AB and O was shown by a pathologist in 1900. Who was he?
(a) Karl Landsteiner (b) Gregor Mendel (c) Joseph Goldberger (d) Alice Hamilton

719. The body derives its energy through the combination of food with oxygen. Who was the French chemist who discovered this?
(a) C. Gay-Lussac (b) Antoine L. Lavoisier (c) Marcelin Berthelot (d) Pierre Curie

720. Who discoverd 'genes' and became the pioneer of the science of Genetics?
(a) Sir James Paget (b) Emil Kraepelin (c) Gregor Mendel (d) John Waksman

721. Who was the first person to see during his studies on anatomy that blood flows through the small blood vessels in the body?
(a) Marcello Malphigi (b) Otto Meyerhof (c) William Harvey (d) Robert Hooke

722. The hereditary factor present in chromosomes is nothing but DNA which is deoxyribonucleic acid. Who discovered the structure of DNA?

(a) Mathias Schleiden (b) John Hilton (c) Anton von Leeuwenhock (d) James D. Watson and Francis H.C. Crick

723. Cholesterol is synthesized from acetic acid in the cells of animals. To which scientist does the credit of this discovery go?
(a) Konrad Emil Block (b) Karl Ernest von Baer (c) Claude Bernard (d) Robert Hooke

724. In 1956, two scientists working in the University of Lund in Sweden proved the number of chromosomes to be 46. Who were they?
(a) Allvar Guilstrand and S.A.S. Urogh (b) Wilhem Einthoven and Christiaan Eijkman (c) J.H.Tjio and A. Levan (d) E.B. Chain and Sir Howard W. Florey

Diseases

725. 'Blue Babies' have a bluish skin because at birth they have a partial blockage of the pulmonary artery. Who discovered this?
(a) Hippocrates (b) Helen Brooke Taussig (c) George Minot (d) Karl Landsteiner

726. Who explained the pathology of appendicitis?
(a) Alexis Carrel (b) Sir Julian Huxley (c) John Hunter (d) Charles H. Best

727. Who was the first to discover that bacteria produces infections in wounds?
(a) Albert Schweitzer (b) Jonas E. Salk (c) Louis Pasteur (d) Karl Pearson

728. The study of beriberi and the importance of Vitamin B_1, was carried out by a Dutch scientist named:
(a) August von Wassermann (b) Robert Hooke (c) John Cheyne (d) Christiaan Eijkman

729. Who was the surgeon who discovered that tuberculosis affects the spine?
(a) Egas Moniz (b) Percival Pott (c) James Lind (d) Antoine Becquerel

730. An English doctor was responsible for studying and explaining the causes of nephritis. Who was he?

(a) Karl Pearson (b) Richard Bright (c) Robert Brown (d) Wilfred Grenfell

731. Who found a cure for scurvy in 1753?

(a) James Lind (b) Sir Charles Lyell (c) Abraham Colles (d) Crawford Long

732. Serious mental ailments occur as a result of the lack of the B group of Vitamins arising out of excess consumption of alcohol. Who was the discoverer of this disease?

(a) A German called Robert Koch (b) A Russian called Sergei Korsakoff (c) A German called Felix Gaisböck (d) An American called Eldon J. Gardner

733. From the following, name the person who undertook studies on Pellagra:

(a) Sir John Tomes (b) A.T. Still (c) Joseph Goldberger (d) John Braxton Hicks

734. Who discovered the organism responsible for the venereal disease chancroid?

(a) Augusto Ducrey (b) Michael E. Debakey (c) Sigmund Freud (d) Franz Mesmer

735. The discoverer of Down's Syndrome in 1866 was J.L. Down. Who was he?

(a) An American doctor (b) A British scientist (c) An American paediatrician (d) A British doctor

736. Who found the cause and cure of rickets?

(a) Watt (b) Cavendish (c) Mellanby (d) Lister

737. Who is the founder of a liver disease which is known by his name?

(a) S.A.K. Wilson (b) Michael De Bakey (c) Christiaan Bernard (d) Wallace M. Yater

738. A German bacteriologist was the first to discover the bacillus responsible for tuberculosis. Who was he?

(a) Gerhard Domagk (b) Robert Koch (c) Samuel Hahnemann (d) Paul Ehrlich

739. In which year did Hodgkin discover the cancerous disease known as Hodgkin's disease?
(a) 1932 (b) 1947 (c) 1837 (d) 1735

740. A French doctor devised the blood test that is used for detecting typhoid. Who was he?
(a) Herman Gartner (b) William Halsted (c) Fernand Widal (d) Hans Geiger

741. A Scottish army surgeon discovered that the carrier of malaria was none other than the Anopheles mosquito. Who was he?
(a) Ronald Ross (b) William Harvey (c) Richard Bright (d) Thomas Addison

742. Who received the 1989 Nobel Prize for medicine for their study of 'viral oncogenes', by which they discovered that damage to genes is responsible for triggering off cancer?
(a) Michael Bishop and Harold Varmus (b) William Harvey and Robert Koch (c) Michael Brown and Joseph Goldslein (d) John Black and Gertrude Elion

Drugs

743. Who was the German scientist who introduced 'chemotherapy' and is known as the father of chemotherapy?
(a) Paul Ehrlich (b) Robert Koch (c) Galen (d) Wilhelm K. Roentgen

744. Who was the discoverer of Penicillin?
(a) Edward Jenner (b) Alexander Fleming (c) Joseph Lister (d) Norman Bethune

745. The first sulfa drug Prontosil was discovered by a German physician. Who was he?
(a) H.A. Krebs (b) August Weismann (c) Gerhard Domagk (d) Paul Ehrlich

746. Who used anaesthetics for the first time during surgery?
(a) William Harvey (b) Richard Bright (c) Ernst B. Chain (d) Crawford Long and William Morton

747. Who isolated griseofulvin from penicillium griseofulvum?
(a) Blackwell (b) Dierck (c) Baer (d) Koch

748. Which scientists were responsible for the conversion of natural penicillin into synthetic penicillin?
(a) Ross and Domagk (b) Sheehan and Ferris (c) Fleming and Chain (d) Gram and Koch

749. Who was the first to introduce antiseptics during surgery?
(a) Joseph Lister (b) Gerhard Domagk (c) Karl Pearson (d) Sir David Bruce

750. Who was the founder of the oral vaccine against poliomyelitis?
(a) Claude Bernard (b) Albert B. Sabin (c) Ascanio Sobrero (d) Rudolf Brenner

751. Who discovered the small-pox vaccination?
(a) Edward Jenner (b) Sir William Jenner (c) Sir Ronald Ross (d) Thomas Addison

752. Who was the first to isolate the antibiotic Chloromycetin?
(a) Robert Burns Woodward (b) Brieger Ludwig (c) Selman A. Waksman (d) Paul Ehrlich

753. Who discovered the teratogenic effect of thalidomide?
(a) Williams (b) Harrison (c) McBride and Lenz (d) Thornton

754. Who isolated the antibiotic Dactinomycin (needed for cancer chemotherapy) in 1940?
(a) Waksman and Woodruff (b) Chain and Florey (c) Ross and Pasteur (d) Lister and Watt

755. Who discovered that the drug streptomycin has antitubercular action?
(a) Mary E. Walker (b) Selman A. Waksman (c) Hermann Rorschach (d) Bela Schick

756. Sulphapyridine, a sulphonamide drug, was introduced in 1938. Who were responsible for its introduction?

(a) Holmes, Bell and Edison (b) Ewins, Whitly and Philips (c) Minot, Koch and Pasteur (d) Morgan, Ross and Tatum

757. In 1910, the first drug with chemotherapeutic activity called Salvarsan was discovered. Who was the discoverer?
(a) Louis Pasteur (b) Robert Koch (c) Paul Ehrlich (d) Daniel H. Williams

Instruments and devices

758. Who is the pioneer in the field of interventional neuroradiology (INR)?
(a) Ivan P. Pavlov (b) Professor Luc Picard (c) John Gorrie (d) Camillo Golgi

759. Who discovered X-ray?
(a) Wilhelm Conrad Roentgen (b) Pierre Curie (c) Marie Curie (d) Irene Curie

760. Who made the first dental X-rays?
(a) Marie Curie (b) Otto Walkhoff (c) A.H. Becquerel (d) Philippe C.E. Gaucher

761. Who is the Russian doctor, who has given a new direction to orthopaedics by inventing a device with which limbs can be lengthened and accident and other deformities corrected?
(a) Edward Flatau (b) Karl Konstantinovich Dehio (c) Gavriil Abramovich Ilizarov (d) Ivan P. Pavlov

762. Who discovered the thermometer?
(a) Issac Newton (b) John Dalton (c) Ronald Ross (d) Galileo Galelei

Miscellaneous

763. Who classified bacteria types into Gram-positive and Gram-negative?
(a) Robert Brown (b) Charles Darwin (c) Christian Gram (d) Paul Ehrlich

764. Who discovered the theory that specific chemical reactions are regulated by genes?

(a) Sigmund Freud (b) Lord Florey (c) Louis Pasteur (d) Edward L. Tatum and George W. Beadle

765. Who was the first to categorize people into extroverts and introverts?
(a) Carl Gustav Jung (b) John J. Macleod (c) Franz Mesmer (d) Julian Huxley

766. Who was the founder of modern nursing?
(a) Elizabeth Blackwell (b) Florence Nightingale (c) Mary S. Calderone (d) Anna H. Shaw

767. Who performed the first heart transplant?
(a) Karl Pearson (b) Christian Bernard (c) Wilfred Grenfell (d) August Weismann

768. Who propounded the 'Theory of Evolution'?
(a) Sir Joseph Lister (b) Charles Darwin (c) Karl E. von Baer (d) Alexander Rollet

769. The fact that microorganisms are living beings and not non-living beings was found by:
(a) Louis Pasteur (b) Alexander Ogston (c) Albert B. Sabin (d) Paul D. White

770. Vitamin D was discovered by:
(a) Stokes (b) Servetus (c) McCollum (d) Finlay

771. Who characterized Vitamin A in 1913?
(a) Sigmund Freud (b) Gregor Mendel (c) William Hey (d) George Minot

772. Who is known as the 'father of medicine'?
(a) Hippocrates (b) Aristotle (c) Socrates (d) Pythagoras

773. Who is the American doctor who discovered osteopathy?
(a) J. Vane (b) Andrew Taylor Still (c) Felix Gaisböck (d) Konrad E. Bloch

774. An entomologist has discovered a protozoan parasite named Microsporidia, which is a mosquito killer. Who is this entomologist?
(a) Carolus Linnaeus (b) Karl von Frisch (c) Tom Sweeney (d) Konrad Lorenz

775. Who was the American doctor who found that plasma from blood can be used for transfusions?
(a) Charles Richard Drew (b) Sidney Howard (c) Paul Ehrlich (d) Rosalyn Yalow

776. The discoverer of bacteria was a Dutch scientist. Who was he?
(a) Karlos Fallopius (b) August von Wassermann (c) Anton von Leeuwenhock (d) Franz Mesmer

777. Who was the medical practitioner who first studied psychiatry in a systematic manner?
(a) Erasistratus (b) Emil Kraepelin (c) A.J. Clark (d) Henry Cavendish

778. In the year 1543, the first textbook dealing with the anatomy of the human body was published. Who was the author of this book?
(a) Gustav Kornberg (b) Charles Darwin (c) Charles H. Best (d) Andreas Versalius

779. Who wrote the book *Omne Vivum Ex Ovo*, in which the author stipulated that all living beings come into existence from an egg?
(a) Alexis Joffroy (b) John Braxton Hicks (c) William Harvey (d) Vladimir Kerwig

780. Who was the founder of the injectable vaccine against poliomyelitis?
(a) Koch (b) Gauss (c) Salk (d) Cavendish

781. Which scientist laid the foundation of embryology?
(a) Philippe Gaucher (b) Eldon Gardner (c) Karl Ernest von Baer (d) Augusto Ducrey

782. *The Origin of Species* is a compilation of whose work?
(a) H. Collier (b) Charles Darwin (c) Halsted (d) Carl J. Gauss

783. In the 1970s a movement opposing and denouncing the use of electro-convulsive therapy on mental patients came into being. Who was the leader of this movement?
(a) John Friedberg (b) John Hilton (c) Alexis Joffroy (d) Karen Horney

784. Which of the following devised an operation of the prostrate?
(a) William Harvey (b) J. William White (c) Henry B. Millard (d) Percival Pott

785. Who is the founder of Orthomolecular psychiatry?
(a) Sigmund Freud (b) Linus Pauling (c) Earnest Jones (d) William James

786. Who laid the basis of Homoeopathy?
(a) Charles Darwin (b) Dmitri Ivanovich Mendeleev (c) Samuel Hahnemann (d) Henry Cavendish

787. Who discovered carbolic acid?
(a) Joseph Lister (b) Henry Cavendish (c) John Dalton (d) Fritz Pregl

10
POLLUTION AND HEALTH

Causes

788. There are many viruses ranging from viruses causing gastroenteritis to viruses causing jaundice that find their way into our system through the water we drink. Can you tell the approximate range within which the sizes of viruses lie?
(a) 550 to 500 nm (b) 650 to 450 nm (c) 300 to 20 nm (d) 900 to 800 nm

789. Cars cause air pollution because they throw out the poisonous gas known as:
(a) Hydrogen (b) Carbon monoxide (c) Carbon dioxide (d) Nitrogen

790. Mercury and particulate matter are thrown into the air by:
(a) Burning garbage (b) Aeroplanes (c) Coal-fired ovens (d) Steam engines

791. Benzene is a solvent that is used in many and varied industries. Which type of cancer does it cause?

(a) Prostate cancer (b) Bone marrow cancer (c) Oral cancer (d) Skin cancer

792. Fungicides, herbicides and insecticides not only destroy pests but they also destroy:
(a) Plants (b) The texture of the soil (c) The useful bacteria present in the soil (d) The nutrients present in the soil

793. For proper hearing a sound level of about 55 decibels is good enough for the human ear. At what decibel of sound does deafness occur by breaking the ear-drum or by causing internal ear injury?
(a) 160 decibels (b) 70 decibels (c) 80 decibels (d) 90 decibels

794. Which of the following represents the latest chemical weapons that are fabricated for mass killing?
(a) Time bombs (b) Bigeye bombs (c) Dynamite (d) Dioxin

795. The 'Greenhouse effect' is predicted to bring about which type of change in the earth?
(a) Rise in temperature (b) Continuous rainfall (c) Lowering of temperature (d) Continuous snowing

796. Air pollution from the air-borne parts of a certain plant causes dermatitis, which requires long-drawn treatment with corticosteroids. Which of the following is this plant?
(a) Rawolfia serpentina (b) Fraxinus americana L (c) Phaseolus vulgaris L (d) Parthenium hysterophorum

797. Experiments have shown that cadmium is harmful to health and may cause hypertension and diseases of the heart. In which of the following is cadmium present?
(a) Exhaust from cars (b) Rain water (c) Cigarette smoke (d) Exhaust from trucks

798. In which of the following fuels is the content of lead the highest?
(a) Coal (b) Cooking gas (c) Low octane petrol (d) High octane petrol

799. When wood preserved with chlorophenols is burnt, the chlorophenols are transformed into poisonous chemicals. What are these known as?
(a) Carbon dioxide (b) Chlorodioxins (c) Nitrogen Dioxide (d) Organotins

800. Which of the following are present in cigarette smoke and are potential carcinogens?
(a) Benzopyrene (b) Phosgene (c) Carbon dioxide (d) Polycyclic hydrocarbons

801. Obnoxious odours of gases released during chemical processes in industries cause a lot of air pollution. Hydrogen sulphide is one such pollutant. These gases can be removed by absorbing them into certain solutions, the process being known as scrubbing. Scrubbing with which of the following solutions will remove hydrogen sulphide?
(a) Caustic solution (b) Ferrous sulphate solution (c) Copper sulphate solution (d) Sodium fluoride solution

802. Lead in water is responsible for which of the following ailments?
(a) Eye damage (b) Loss of hair (c) Kidney damage (d) Arthritis

803. Which one of the following chemicals is used to increase the octane number of petrol?
(a) Butane (b) Octane (c) Benzene (d) Tetraethyl lead

Ill effects

804. Polluted air has floating particles which cause:
(a) Chicken pox (b) Rubella (c) Measles (d) Bronchitis and asthma

805. Air pollution from the leakage of Methyl Isocyanate gas from the factory of Union Carbide

in Bhopal caused a major tragedy. When did this take place?

(a) 3 December 1984 (b) 15 December 1983 (c) 7 December 1982 (d) 8 December 1981

806. Sewage water is a potential source of many bacterial diseases ranging from cholera, dysentery, tuberculosis and typhoid. To which group can the bacteria causing cholera be categorised?

(a) Shigella (b) Vibrio (c) Staphylococcus (d) Streptococcus

807. Methyl mercury is a dangerous pollutant that causes brain damage and mostly finds its way into the human system through consumption of contaminated fish. How does it affect a pregnant woman?

(a) The woman becomes very weak and has difficult labour. (b) The woman loses her memory completely, but the child is born healthy (c) The woman delivers prematurely, followed by a lot of complications (d) Instead of harming the woman, methyl mercury harms the unborn child by accumulating in its brain

808. Many people died in London in 1952 as a result of air pollution producing:

(a) Mist (b) Smog (c) Fog (d) Sleet

809. Which of the following is harmed when people inhale mercury present in the air?

(a) Hair (b) Nails (c) Skin (d) Nervous system

810. It has been found that bacteria, fungi and certain fishes convert the relatively less harmful mercury compounds present or released in the environment into the more dangerous methyl mercury. Which of the following fungi has been found to make methyl mercury?

(a) Actinomyces bovis (b) Aspergillus fumigatus (c) Aspergillus flavus (d) Neurospora crassa

811. Oil spillage from storage tanks and other sources is a major source of oil pollution of drinking

water supplies. How can the pollution be prevented after such a spillage?

(a) By ordinary osmosis (b) By reverse osmosis (c) By electro-osmosis (d) By polarography

812. Oxides of nitrogen present in air undergo complex chemical reactions in the presence of sunlight to produce another air pollutant. Which is that?

(a) Hydrogen fluoride (b) Sulphur dioxide (c) Hydrocyanic acid gas (d) Ozone

813. Sulphur dioxide is a dangerous air pollutant and harms plant life. What changes in the plant indicate its toxic effect?

(a) Darkening of the leaves (b) Withering of the leaves (c) Falling of leaves (d) Bleaching of the leaves

814. Which one of the following plants or trees can be used as a biomonitor for sulphur dioxide?

(a) Pine tree (b) Alfalfa plant (c) Rose plant (d) Mango tree

815. Consumption of fish thriving in water polluted with mercury can cause:

(a) Death (b) Epilepsy (c) Down's syndrome (d) Gastric ulcer

816. Which of the following is a silent killer gas which combines with haemoglobin in the blood?

(a) Carbon dioxide (b) Nitrogen dioxide (c) Nitric oxide (d) Carbon monoxide

817. Scientists working at the Applied Marine Research Laboratory in the Netherlands have found that the hatching and laying of eggs by ducks are severely affected by pollution. Which are these pollutants?

(a) Pesticides (b) Fertilizers (c) Insect-infested grains (d) Dirt

818. The pesticides DDT and BHC have been found to be:

(a) Allergens (b) Carcinogens (c) Asthmatic agents (d) Pathogens

819. Leaves of grapes plant are affected by air pollution from ozone. How can the injury be detected?
(a) The leaves are bleached (b) The leaves develop holes (c) The leaves develop black or purple spots (d) The leaves shrink in size

820. Which one of the following methods is used to separate organic pollutants from water?
(a) Crystallisation (b) Reverse osmosis (c) Precipitation (d) Column chromatography

821. Which part of the body is usually damaged from lead poisoning?
(a) Kidney (b) Heart (c) Brain (d) Lungs

822. Which one of the following is responsible for damaging blood?
(a) Lead (b) Arsenic (c) Calcium (d) Magnesium

823. A severe case of mercury poisoning surfaced itself when some Japanese consumed tuna fish polluted with methyl mercury. What was this disease?
(a) Cholera (b) Food poisoning (c) Minamata disease (d) Liver cancer

824. Chemicals and radiations have been found to bring about changes in which of the following?
(a) Hair (b) Chromosomes (c) Nails (d) Height of a person

825. Which one of the following radioisotope contaminant present in dairy products and cereals is mistakenly used by the body, thereby causing cancer of the bone marrow?
(a) Potassium 40 (b) Uranium 235 (c) Strontium 90 (d) Uranium 236

826. Which of the following is not only a carcinogen but a potential cause of brain damage as well?
(a) Fluorine (b) Methyl mercury (c) Chlorine (d) Cobalt

827. Which of the following are the carcinogenic chemicals present in the smoke of wood?
(a) Benzopyrene (b) Sulphur dioxide (c) Nitrogen peroxide (d) Polycyclic hydrocarbons

828. Which one of the following is produced when carbon monoxide combines with haemoglobin of blood?
(a)   Haemopexin   (b)   Carboxyhaemoglobin
(c) Hemotoglobulin (d) Oxyhaemoglobin

Miscellaneous
829. Which of the following are employed nowadays to remove wastes from water?
(a) Virus (b) Bacteria (c) Fish (d) Porpoises
830. Floating particles of dirt, moss, etc., in water can be settled by adding:
(a) Calcium carbonate (b) Calcium phosphate
(c) Alum (d) Barium hydroxide
831. Harmful germs in water can be killed by passing through it:
(a) Chlorine gas (b) Oxygen gas (c) Hydrogen gas
(d) Carbon dioxide
832. Which of the following plants or trees will be a potential source of insecticides in the near future?
(a) Mango (b) Neem (c) Eucalyptus (d) Tobacco
833. Biological pollutants are also a potential source of air pollution and cause diseases. Meningitis is caused by an organism known as Neisseria meningetidis. To which of the following categories does it belong?
(a) Virus (b) Fungus (c) Bacteria (d) Parasite
834. Polychlorinated biphenyls used in transformers and capacitors are a hazardous group of organic compounds. Which one of the following methods can be employed for their disposal from wastes?
(a) Filtration through membrane filters (b) Distillation under vacuum (c) Crystallisation in special solvents (d) Combustion in specially designed kilns
835. Aromatic amines and phenols arising out of the dyes, plastics, petroleum refining and many other industries pose a great threat to human health. Which of the following do they cause?

(a) Meningitis (b) Food poisoning (c) Cancer (d) Typhoid

836. Which one of the following methods can be used to remove aromatic amines and phenols from waste water?
(a) Use of combustion (b) Use of filtration (c) Use of co-precipitation (d) Use of microbes

837. Poisonous gases like hydrogen cyanide and cyanogen chloride cause the respiratory system to fail. They are known as:
(a) Blood gases (b) Sewer gases (c) Distention gases (d) Inflammable gases

838. Which one of the following days is observed as World Environment Day every year?
(a) 5 May (b) 5 June (c) 18 July (d) 6 April

839. Methyl isocyanate, phosgene, etc., are some of the harmful raw materials that are required to manufacture:
(a) Pesticides and chemical weapons (b) Fertilizers (c) Paints (d) Solvents

840. Which one of the following is a common pesticide?
(a) Chloroform (b) Malathion (c) Benzene (d) Carbon tetrachloride

841. Which fumigant is used to protect foodgrains during storage?
(a) DDT (b) Aluminium phosphide (c) Folidol (d) 2-isopropoxyphenyl methyl carbamate

842. Which of the following pesticides is banned in the USA?
(a) DDT (b) Methyl parathion (c) Toxaphene (d) Malathion

843. Compared to the population of the rest of the world, which of the following is found in high concentration in the body of an Indian?
(a) Calcium (b) Sodium (c) Potassium (d) DDT

844. Milk sold in Maharashtra has been found to have residues of:

(a) DDT and dieldrin (b) Chlordane (c) Heptachlor (d) Endrin

845. The unit that is used to measure noise is known as:

(a) Joule (b) Decibels (c) Percentage (d) Volts

846. How many decibels of noise can be tolerated by the human ear?

(a) About 20 decibels (b) About 150 decibels (c) About 80 decibels (d) About 120 decibels

847. What is the chemical name for tear gas?

(a) DDT (b) Carbon disulfide (c) Sulphur dioxide (d) Chloropicrin

848. Tobacco is not only used in cigarettes, but is chewed by many people. Which is the poisonous alkaloid that is present in tobacco?

(a) Elaeocarpine (b) Nicotine (c) Atropine (d) Strychnine

849. From which year, cigarette packets sold in the USA carried the label warning against risk to health?

(a) January 1966 (b) January 1973 (c) March 1970 (d) February 1985

850. From the following chemicals which are the ones that are used to preserve wood?

(a) DDT (b) Alcohol (c) Chlorophenols (d) Methanol

851. New Delhi has been found to have less noise pollution compared to Bombay because:

(a) There are many public gardens where the shouts of children get confined (b) The air has less vibration (c) Buildings have acoustic walls to absorb the noise (d) There is less congestion and there are trees on the sides of the roads which absorb the sound

852. Do you know how much noise you are generating by turning on your TV to the maximum volume?

(a) About 25 decibels (b) 18 decibels or may be less (c) About 65 decibels (d) About 5 decibels

853. Improper use of antibiotics to protect poultry and domestic animals is harmful. Why?
(a) Because this results in antibiotic residues in their body which may harm human beings who consume them or their products (b) Because this may make them age faster (c) Because this may make them thinner (d) Antibiotics affect the shells of eggs, the feather of birds and the fur of animals

854. Vegetables grown by the roadside have a higher content of:
(a) Lead (b) Calcium (c) Iron (d) Vitamins

11
REMEDIES

Surgical

855. The use of very low temperatures during surgery is known as:
(a) Cryosurgery (b) Microtomy (c) Conservative surgery (d) Aseptic surgery

856. Ischaemia, which results from the blocked coronary artery, can be corrected by:
(a) Baccelli's operation (b) Splenectomy (c) Brasdor's operation (d) Bypass surgery

857. To make the heart beat at a steady rate the instrument that is implanted near the heart is known as:
(a) Cardioscope (b) Cardiometer (c) Pacemaker (d) Cardiophone

858. What is the terminology used for an operation involving the nervous system?
(a) Neurosurgery (b) Angioplasty (c) Iridotomy (d) Neuroplasty

859. When surgery of the heart and lungs are resorted to, what is it known as?
(a) Pulmonary surgery (b) Thoracic surgery (c) Microsurgery (d) Neurotomy

860. Which one of the following is used in laparoscopic surgery?
(a) Pneumograph (b) Argon laser (c) Yag laser (d) Labidometer

861. Many successful operations of the retina and operations inside the abdomen have been carried out with:
(a) Argon laser (b) Liquid lasers (c) Helium-Neon laser (d) Carbon dioxide laser

862. Which one of the following operations is done on patients suffering from varicose veins?
(a) Emmet's operation (b) Babcock's surgery (c) Lobectomy (d) Stapedectomy

863. Cingulotomy is an operation that is performed on:
(a) Heart patients (b) Cancer patients (c) Mental patients (d) Pregnant women

864. In order to remove malignant tumours from the breast, the breast is removed surgically. What is this operation known as?
(a) Mastectomy (b) Fricke's operation (c) Hibb's operation (d) Cowell's operation

865. In which of the following operations is the uterus removed?
(a) Woelfler's operation (b) Phelp's operation (c) Mikulicz's operation (d) Hysterectomy

866. Often the birth of children is brought about by an incision on the abdomen. What is this commonly known as?
(a) Forceps delivery (b) Caesarean section (c) Woelfler's operation (d) Chrymar's operation

867. When one of the lobes of a lung is removed by surgical operation, it is known as:
(a) Lobectomy (b) Tarsectomy (c) Lobotomy (d) Lung removal

868. Patients suffering from schizophrenia and who fail to respond to other modes of therapy are given relief by an operation known as:

113

(a) Leucotomy (b) Laparotomy (c) Watkin's operation (d) Gastroenterostomy

869. In cataract surgery which one of the following is used?
(a) YAG laser (b) IR rays (c) Ruby laser (d) Semiconductor lasers

870. For what is the operation known as 'phakoemulsification' performed?
(a) To remove tumour of the larynx (b) To remove a cataract from the eye (c) To remove a kidney (d) To remove gall stones

871. The appendix is removed in acute appendicitis to give relief to the patient. What is this operation known as?
(a) Angioplasty (b) Richter's operation (c) Witzel's operation (d) Ecphyadectomy

872. When the entire colon is removed surgically, the operation is known as:
(a) Total lobotomy (b) Total colectomy (c) Transplantation (d) Total proctotomy

873. An operation by which the cut end of the small intestine is attached to the skin of the abdomen and a bag is attached to the opening to collect the excreta is known as:
(a) Ileostomy (b) Pubetrotomy (c) Testectomy (d) Urethrostomy

874. A sharp surgical equipment is used for cutting bones. What is it called?
(a) Knife (b) Enterotome (c) Orthoscope (d) Osteotome

875. In breast cancer sometimes the entire breast is removed by surgery. What is this operation?
(a) Biotomy (b) Breast surgery (c) Percy's operation (d) Radial mastectomy

876. Ugliness of different parts of the body can be corrected with the help of:
(a) Rau's operation (b) Cosmetic surgery (c) Dowell's operation (d) Cryosurgery

877. Which of the following involves surgery of the foot?
(a) Glossectomy (b) Lithotomy (c) Chiloplasty
(d) Mikulicz's operation

878. Which of the following operations is carried out on patients suffering from peptic ulcer?
(a) Enterotomy (b) Vagotomy (c) Hysterectomy
(d) Buck's operation

879. Which of the following operations is used to rectify a club foot?
(a) Tenoplasty (b) Stapedectomy (c) Plastic surgery (d) Phelp's operation

880. When there is a tumour in the larynx, which of the following operations is resorted to?
(a) Rossbach's operation (b) White's operation
(c) Woelfler's operation (d) McDowell's operation

881. Which of the following involves an operation of the ear?
(a) Vasostomy (b) Cochlear implant
(c) Neurotomy (d) Nephrectomy

882. By which of the following methods can tumours be destroyed?
(a) Infrared rays (b) Ultraviolet rays (c) Ultrasonic waves (d) Surgical diathermy

883. Which of the following operations is resorted to in order to remove a tumour from the ovary?
(a) Vasectomy (b) Oariotomy (c) Lithotomy
(d) Celiotomy

884. When plastic surgery is done on the stomach what is it referred to as?
(a) Stomatoplasty (b) Nymphectomy
(c) Gastroplasty (d) Luke's operation

885. When plastic surgery is performed on the nose and the upper portion of the lip, what is it known as?
(a) Angioplasty (b) Rhinochiloplasty (c) Maloplasty (d) Cirsectomy

886. Which of the following is the latest technique in the treatment of malformations of the arteries and veins in the nervous system?
(a) Interventional neuroradiology (b) Neurotomy (c) Gastroplasty (d) Tachography

887. Which of the following is used to control uraemia?
(a) Diathermy (b) Nephropexy (c) Dialysis (d) Kehr's operation

888. Which of the following is a remedy by which the painful part of the body is massaged and moved gently into correct position?
(a) Osteopathy (b) Mechanotherapy (c) Acupuncture (d) Acupressure

889. One of the techniques in the treatment of cervical cancer involves destroying the cancerous cells by vaporizing them in a short time. Which technique is this?
(a) Uteroplasty (b) Use of carbon dioxide laser (c) Uterotomy (d) Use of cervimeter

890. Which one of the following refers to the treatment of mental diseases with the help of electric shocks?
(a) Electroscission (b) Electrography (c) Electrothermotherapy (d) Electroconvulsive therapy

891. Which of the following treatments tones up the muscles and improves circulation?
(a) Massage (b) Electrolysis (c) Spasmolysis (d) Skin peeling

892. A treatment is resorted to, by which muscle pains and strains and problems of the joints are relieved, by generating heat energy below the skin. What is the name of this treatment?
(a) Osteoplasty (b) Diathermy (c) Thermometry (d) Thermocautery

893. A machine is used nowadays to give relief to patients suffering from chronic arthritis. Which is this machine?

116

(a) Osteoscope (b) NMR machine (c) Thermograph (d) Transcutaneous electrical nerve stimulator

894. A method by which eggs from the ovaries of a woman who cannot conceive are collected, fertilized outside the body and planted back into the woman's womb to make her pregnant is known as:

(a) Pubiotomy (b) Laparohysteropexy (c) Laparoscopy (d) In-vitro fertilization and embryo transfer (IVF-ET)

895. A method by which a woman can conceive by implanting the sperm and the egg into the woman's uterus with the help of laparoscopy is known as:

(a) Laparocolotomy (b) Laparocystotomy (c) Laparo-uterotomy (d) Gamete intra-fallopian transfer (GIFT)

896. Which of the following is the latest technique employed to remove wrinkles from the face?

(a) Arterioplasty (b) Waxing (c) Bleaching (d) Collagen implant

897. Excessive fat in the body is removed by suction. What is the technique known as?

(a) Lipolysis (b) Electrolysis (c) Dialysis (d) Lipectomy

898. Which instrument is used to break the stones in the bladder into small pieces and then remove them from there?

(a) Lithotome (b) Lithotriptoscope (c) Lithophone (d) Lithometer

12
DENTISTRY

General Information

899. The front teeth help us to cut our food. What are these known as?
(a) Incisors (b) Molars (c) Canines (d) Premolars

900. Which of the following do teeth contain?
(a) Sodium (b) Calcium (c) Potassium (d) Iron

901. How many teeth including the wisdom teeth does an adult person have?
(a) Twenty-eight (b) Thirty-two (c) Thirty (d) Twenty-nine

902. To break up sticky food and for tearing food a particular type of teeth are used. These are situated next to the incisors. What are these called?
(a) Canines (b) Incisors (c) Premolars (d) Wisdom teeth

903. Which of the following are used to grind our food?
(a) Canines (b) Incisors (c) Premolars (d) Wisdom teeth

904. In which category will you place the wisdom teeth?
(a) Molars (b) Canines (c) Incisors (d) Premolars

905. Which of the following is used by a dentist topically for fluoride treatment?
(a) Solution of silver difluoride (b) Solution of calcium fluoride (c) Solution of sodium fluoride (d) Solution of cobalt trifluoride

906. A disagreeable smell emanates from many people's mouth. What is this condition known as?
(a) Halitosis (b) Candidiasis (c) Periodontitis (d) Dentinitis

907. Often the surface of the teeth gets covered with a hard mass of calcium salts. What is this known as?
(a) Tartar (b) Plaque (c) Caries (d) Calculus

908. Which teeth are the last to appear?

(a) Incisors (b) Wisdom teeth (c) Canines
(d) Premolars

909. In which of the following does the protective enamel present on the teeth dissolve out?
(a) Acid medium (b) Alkaline medium (c) Hard water (d) Soft water

910. Bacterial growth are found in the plaque on teeth. These bacteria convert carbohydrates in food to a certain acid which dissolves the protective enamel present on teeth. Which acid is this?
(a) Citric acid (b) Lactic acid (c) Aceticacid (d) Ascorbic acid

Diseases

911. The presence of excess fluoride in the body causes damage to the bones and teeth. What is this disease known as?
(a) Fluorosis (b) Arthritis (c) Silicosis (d) Osteosarcoma

912. In which of the following is there inflammation of the gums?
(a) Glossitis (b) Stomatitis (c) Gingivitis (d) Tonsillitis

913. The surface of the teeth gets covered with a film as a result of the formation of colonies by microorganisms. What is this known as?
(a) Gingivitis (b) Plaque (c) Caries (d) Granuloma

914. To which of the following does Dentalgia refer to?
(a) Small size of teeth (b) Improper oral hygiene
(c) Headache arising from tooth trouble
(d) Toothache

915. Which of the following can occur due to a deficiency of Vitamin C?
(a) Osteomalacia (b) Blood poisoning (c) Bleeding of gums (d) Bleeding of nose

916. When should patients with oral cancer have a dental check-up and, if necessary, treatment with fluoride done?
(a) After radiotherapy (b) Before radiotherapy (c) After chemotherapy (d) After surgery

917. How can one prevent dental caries?
(a) By adequate intake of fluorine (b) By including a proper amount of calcium in diet and maintaining good oral hygiene (c) By eating lots of fruit (d) By taking a fibre-rich diet

918. A common practice in the West is to use a particular type of thread to clean the space between two teeth. What is this practice known as?
(a) Dental floss (b) Dental cleaning (c) Dentalgia (d) Dental flora

919. Silicate is used for filling dental cavities. To which of the following categories does it belong?
(a) Hydraulic mortar (b) Roman cement (c) Portland cement (d) Porcelain cement

920. Which branch of dentistry corrects the irregular and bad positioning of teeth?
(a) Periodontics (b) Prosthodontics (c) Endodontics (d) Orthodontics

921. Which of the following toothbrushes should be used by a person suffering from bleeding gums?
(a) Soft (b) Hard (c) Medium (d) Angular

922. How often should one change a toothbrush?
(a) After one month (b) After two months (c) When the brush starts losing its shape and starts wearing out (d) After six months

923. Why should we avoid keeping pickles and other sour food in the mouth for long?
(a) Because the food will lose its taste (b) Because saliva destroys sour food (c) Because the acid present in sour food dissolves the enamel

(d) Because there is danger of the occurrence of stomatitis

13
DISEASES AFFLICTING INDUSTRIAL WORKERS

924. Workers employed in industries making mirror and thermometer suffer from:
(a) Mercury poisoning (b) Colitis (c) Lead poisoning (d) Whipple's disease

925. A disease commonly seen in miners of rocks in which they suffer from cough and shortness of breath is known as:
(a) Ankylostomiasis (b) Silicosis (c) Nystagmus (d) Miner's asthma

926. Coal miners inhale dust and as a result suffer from certain diseases which affect the lungs. What are these diseases known as?
(a) Pneumoconiosis (b) Pulmonary congestion (c) Dochmiasis (d) Tuberculosis

927. What is the other name of the disease silicosis?'
(a) Plummer's disease (b) Dyspnoea (c) Miner's anaemia (d) Grinder's asthma

928. Workers employed in industries where asbestos is used should take proper precautions against dust from asbestos to avoid asbestosis. What is asbestosis?
(a) A liver disease (b) A kidney disease (c) A lung disease (d) A mental disease

929. Farmers, gardeners and other workers employed in cultivation are exposed to pollen and other allergy-causing particles in the air. Some develop a nasal disorder as a result of this. Which is this disease?
(a) Gardner-Diamond syndrome (b) Hay fever (c) Sinusitis (d) Anosmia

930. Persons subjected to long-drawn exposure to cotton dust may develop cough and breathing difficulties like asthmatic patients. What is this disease known as?
(a) Silicosis (b) Edward's syndrome (c) Byssinosis (d) Atelectasis

931. Workers working in factories making fluorescent lamps suffer from lung diseases from exposure to:
(a) Radium (b) Beryllium (c) Plutonium (d) Copper

932. Due to excessive perspiration people working near the blast furnace may suffer from:
(a) Iron deficiency (b) Calcium deficiency (c) Sodium deficiency (d) Vitamin deficiency

933. Overexposure to which one of the following makes industrial workers suffer from loss of hair, and a garlicky breath?
(a) Selenium (b) Chlorine (c) Nitric acid (d) Benzene

934. Industrial workers who work under conditions of high temperature may suffer from:
(a) Toothache (b) Heat Cramps (c) Protein deficiency (d) Stomach ache

14
OLD AGE AND ITS AILMENTS

935. In old age the walls of the chest become rigid and the capacity of the lungs decreases, giving rise to difficulty in breathing and shortness of breath. What is this known as?
(a) Pleurisy (b) Dyspepsia (c) Dyspnoea (d) Adenoma

936. Hypertension in old age is due to:

(a) Thickening of the arteries (b) Thickening of the lungs (c) Thickening of the bones (d) Thickening of the heart walls

937. What happens to the skin in old age?
(a) Pigmentation decreases (b) Pigmentation increases (c) Pigmentation remains the same (d) Vitiligo occurs

938. Why is it that old people get fractures easily?
(a) Because bones become soft (b) Because bones have excess phosphates (c) Because bones have excess Vitamin D (d) Because bones become weak due to decalcification

939. Why is diarrhoea common among old people?
(a) Because of reduced hydrochloric acid in the gastric juice and poor hygiene (b) Because of overeating (c) Because of insomnia (d) Because of eating fried food

940. The elastic tissues around the joints become fibrous in old age. How does this affect the movements of the aged?
(a) They become shaky (b) They become stiff and slow (c) They lose interest in walking (d) They cannot stand for long

941. Many aged people suffer from insomnia. To sleep well, what type of a diet should they take before sleeping?
(a) Protein-rich diet (b) Oily food (c) Diet rich in carbohydrates (d) Light carbohydrate meal

942. Which one of the following diseases is likely to strike elderly people suffering from chronic constipation?
(a) Diverticulitis (b) Gastric ulcer (c) Liver trouble (d) Appendicitis

943. Which of the following is a mental disease that gives rise to a loss of memory because of abnormal changes in the brain due to old age?
(a) Sturge-Weber disease (b) Alzheimer's disease (c) Illusion (d) Rud syndrome

944. Why do old people become more prone to diseases than young people?
(a) Because the power of the body's immune system lessens and it fails to recognize the disease germs and fight them (b) Because the power of digestion decreases in old people (c) Because old people lose their self-confidence (d) Because old people forget to take medicines regularly

945. The central vision of the eye gets gradually destroyed on ageing. What is this condition known as?
(a) Trachoma (b) Iridoparalysis (c) Detachment of retina (d) Maculopathy

946. Which of the following do many old people suffer from?
(a) Filaria (b) Chronic bronchitis (c) Migraine (d) Hypochondria

947. Why do tissues of the body get a reduced blood supply in old age?
(a) Because the arteries become hard (b) Because of anaemia (c) Because the arteries become soft (d) Because the heart pumps blood irregularly

948. Diabetes in old age should be properly controlled, otherwise it will leave a wound unhealed, which can lead to:
(a) Chilblain (b) Dermatitis (c) Fungal infection (d) Gangrene

949. Which one of the following manifests itself as one approaches middle age?
(a) Shortsightedness (b) Longsightedness (c) Astigmatism (d) Conjunctivitis

950. As age increases the ability to hear decreases. What is it known as?
(a) Senility (b) Ear defect (c) Presbyacusis (d) Otomycosis

15

MENTAL HEALTH

951. People who suffer from a faulty memory and fail to remember anything are said to be suffering from:
(a) Dementia (b) Mania (c) Phobia (d) Paranoia

952. What is a person who is always worried and depressed about his own health known as?
(a) Kleptomaniac (b) Hypochondriac (c) Abulomaniac (d) Philopatridomaniac

953. Which of the following does a patient suffer from when he loses his memory and fails to remember the past due to some shock, disease or injury?
(a) Nyctophobia (b) Aeroneurosis (c) Anergasin (d) Amnesia

954. In which of the following diseases do old people fail to remember happenings, events or other things?
(a) Hypomania (b) Senile dementia (c) Glioma (d) Parkinson's disease

955. In which of the following does a person's personality get affected and causes disorderly thinking, behaviour, and feelings?
(a) Ataxia (b) Schizophrenia (c) Dementia (d) Transvestism

956. What is the other terminology for schizophrenia?
(a) Strong personality (b) Weak personality (c) Split personality (d) Hysteria

957. In which of the following diseases does the memory become worse day by day followed by bewilderment?
(a) Epiloia (b) Megalocephaly (c) Briquet's syndrome (d) Wernicke's syndrome

958. It is now known that the presence of an extra chromosome causes mental retardation. What is this disease known as?

(a) Phenylketonuria (b) Mongolism (Down's syndrome) (c) Tay-Sachs disease (d) Lesch-nyhan syndrome

959. Mothers suffering from German measles or rubella have been found to give birth to:
(a) Mentally retarded children (b) Rubella inflicted children (c) Children suffering from jaundice (d) Children suffering from typhoid

960. Which of the following is an operation that is carried out on patients suffering from acute schizophrenia?
(a) Vagotomy (b) Vasectomy (c) Osteopathy (d) Leucotomy

961. Which of the following is a genetic disease?
(a) Cerebritis (b) Glioma (c) Encephalopathic syndrome (d) Huntington's disease

962. Which is the disease of middle age in which parts of the brain known as cerebrum gets destroyed?
(a) Hallucination (b) Encephalitis (c) Meningitis (d) Huntington's disease

963. Mental retardation has been found to be associated with the X-chromosome being abnormal. What is the name of this disease?
(a) Reye's syndrome (b) Fragile - X syndrome (c) Microcephaly (d) Tay-Sachs disease

964. Some people suffer from long bouts of sadness and frustration, sometimes leading to suicidal tendencies. In some cases they have to be treated with drugs or electric shock. What is this disease known as?
(a) Depression (b) Dementia (c) Cephaloplegia (d) Aerumna

965. What type of people are megalomaniacs?
(a) Those who have delusions of persecution (b) Those who are stubborn (c) Those who have delusions of riches and power (d) Those who suffer from fear

966. When a person starts staunchly believing in something that is not true he is said to be a victim of:
(a) Melancholia (b) Hysteria (c) Delusion (d) Phobia

967. Which of the following may be a cause for a patient suffering from psychic trauma?
(a) Mental fog (b) Emotional shock (c) Mania (d) Schizoid fantasy

968. In which of the following diseases does the presence of an extra chromosome lead to mental retardation, skeletal dis-figurement and high risk of diabetes mellitus?
(a) Amnesia (b) Hydrocephalus (c) Klinefelter syndrome (d) Lesch-nyhan syndrome

969. When a person is afraid of open places, he is said to be suffering from:
(a) Agoraphobia (b) Hydrophobia (c) Photophobia (d) Ailurophobia

970. A mental disease in which a person gets delusions of torture is known as:
(a) Epilepsy (b) Depression (c) Paranoia (d) Delirium

971. Certain studies have shown scientists that schizophrenia may be due to the presence of a chemical in excess quantity in the brain. Which is this chemical?
(a) Norepinephrine (b) Dopamine (c) Keratin (d) Phenylalanine

972. When a person is afraid of closed areas, he is said to be suffering from:
(a) Megalomania (b) Claustrophobia (c) Autophobia (d) Rhabdophobia

973. When a person tries to remember something, certain changes take place in his brain. In which part of the brain do these changes occur?
(a) Cerebellum (b) Hippocampus (c) Pons (d) Medulla oblongata

974. Can you believe that some people suffer from a strong belief that they have been changed into a cat? What is this known as?
(a) Bell's disease (b) Monomania (c) Hypomania (d) Galeanthropy

975. What is the IQ level of an average individual?
(a) About 50 (b) About 150 (c) About 25 (d) None of the above

16
VISUALS

976. It is the structure of a very common Vitamin used in the prevention and treatment of scurvy. Which is this Vitamin?

977. It is the structure of a very common sedative. Which one is it?

978. It is the structure of a common drug having pain-killing and temperature-reducing properties; but it is not recommended for patients with peptic ulcer. Which is this drug?

979. It is the structure of another very common drug which has pain-killing and temperature-reducing properties. Which is this drug?

980. It is the structure of a drug called Isoniazid. It is used in the treatment of which disease?

981. It is the structure of Niacinamide, a common Vitamin. To which group of Vitamins does it belong?

982. It is the structure of a drug that is used in the treatment of leprosy. Which is this drug?

983. It is the structure of an antibiotic that is used in the treatment of typhoid. Which is this antibiotic?

984. It is the structure of a very common Vitamin which is present in rice. Which is this Vitamin?

985. It is the structure of Penicillin G. Which type of a drug is it?

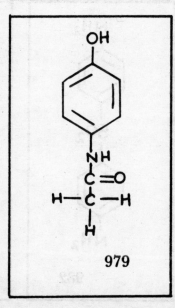

976

977

978

979

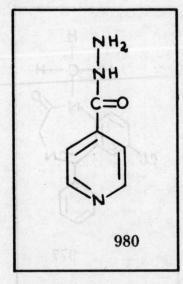

980

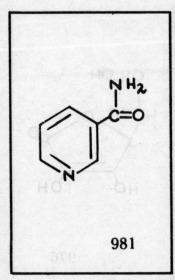

981

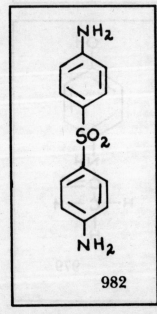

982

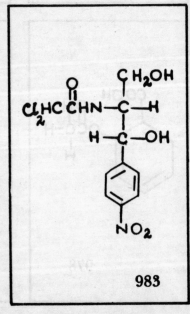

983

984

985

986

987

988

989

990

991

992

993

994

995

996

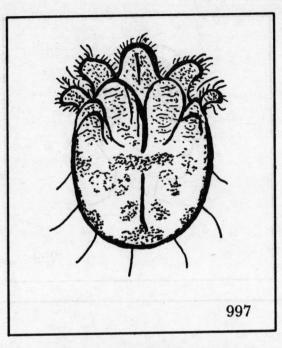

997

998

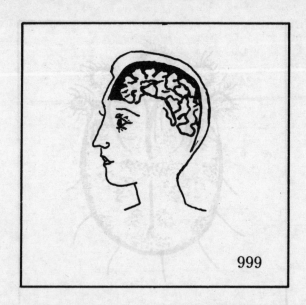

999

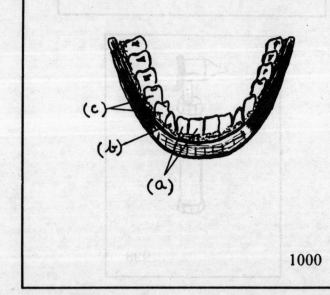

(c)

(b)

(a)

1000

986. It is the structure of Sulphadiazine, a common sulpha drug. Which type of a drug is it?

987. It is the structure of Chlorambucil, an anti-cancer drug. It is used in the treatment of which disease?

988. It is the structure of a common anti-malarial drug. Which is this drug?

989. It is the structure of an anthelmintic drug prescribed by doctors against worm infestations. Which is this drug?

990. It is the structure of a local anaesthetic. Which is that anaesthetic?

991. It is the structure of a thyroid hormone. Which one is it?

992. It is the structure of Ampicillin. What type of a drug is it?

993. It is the structure of a B group of Vitamins, the deficiency of which causes beriberi. Which is this Vitamin?

994. It is the structure of a very common pain-killer. Which one is it?

995. It is the structure of a common red-coloured antiseptic that is applied on cuts and wounds. Which is that antiseptic?

996. It is the structure of an antifungal antibiotic. Which one is it?

997. It is a mite called Sarcoptes scabiei. Which disease does it cause?

998. It is an instrument used for examining the ears. What is it known as?

999. The figure shows the part of the brain that decides our intelligence and memory. Which is this part?

1000. The figure shows the different types of teeth possessed by a human being. What are the names given to (a), (b) and (c) types of teeth?

ANSWERS

1. (c)	2. (b)	3. (a)	4. (b)	5. (a)
6. (c)	7. (d)	8. (a)	9. (b)	10. (a)
11. (b)	12. (d)	13. (b)	14. (a)	15. (a)
16. (b)	17. (b)	18. (d)	19. (b)	20. (b)
21. (d)	22. (a)	23. (b)	24. (c)	25. (b)
26. (b)	27. (a)	28. (b)	29. (a)	30. (b)
31. (b)	32. (c)	33. (a)	34. (b)	35. (d)
36. (a)	37. (b)	38. (a)	39. (d)	40. (c)
41. (b)	42. (a)	43. (a)	44. (d)	45. (c)
46. (b)	47. (c)	48. (c)	49. (a)	50. (b)
51. (c)	52. (c)	53. (b)	54. (c)	55. (b)
56. (a)	57. (b)	58. (d)	59. (c)	60. (d)
61. (d)	62. (c)	63. (a)	64. (c)	65. (a)
66. (a)	67. (c)	68. (c)	69. (b)	70. (a)
71. (b)	72. (a)	73. (b)	74. (c)	75. (c)
76. (d)	77. (a)	78. (d)	79. (b)	80. (b)
81. (c)	82. (d)	83. (a)	84. (a)	85. (d)
86. (c)	87. (b)	88. (a)	89. (c)	90. (d)
91. (b)	92. (a)	93. (a)	94. (c)	95. (b)
96. (a)	97. (c)	98. (b)	99. (a)	100. (c)
101. (c)	102. (a)	103. (a)	104. (b)	105. (c)
106. (a)	107. (b)	108. (a)	109. (d)	110. (c)
111. (a)	112. (b)	113. (c)	114. (d)	115. (b)
116. (a)	117. (b)	118. (c)	119. (a)	120. (b)
121. (c)	122. (a)	123. (d)	124. (c)	125. (a)
126. (d)	127. (a)	128. (c)	129. (c)	130. (a)
131. (b)	132. (c)	133. (a)	134. (d)	135. (a)
136. (c)	137. (a)	138. (a)	139. (c)	140. (a)

141. (d)	142. (a)	143. (b)	144. (a)	145. (b)
146. (b)	147. (a)	148. (c)	149. (b)	150. (b)
151. (a)	152. (c)	153. (b)	154. (b)	155. (a)
156. (c)	157. (a)	158. (b)	159. (d)	160. (b)
161. (b)	162. (c)	163. (a)	164. (b)	165. (c)
166. (b)	167. (a)	168. (b)	169. (c)	170. (a)
171. (b)	172. (d)	173. (b)	174. (a)	175. (b)
176. (a)	177. (b)	178. (c)	179. (a)	180. (b)
181. (d)	182. (b)	183. (c)	184. (b)	185. (c)
186. (b)	187. (a)	188. (a)	189. (b)	190. (a)
191. (b)	192. (a)	193. (c)	194. (c)	195. (a)
196. (b)	197. (a)	198. (b)	199. (a)	200. (a)
201. (d)	202. (d)	203. (a)	204. (c)	205. (b)
206. (a)	207. (b)	208. (b)	209. (a)	210. (d)
211. (a)	212. (c)	213. (d)	214. (c)	215. (d)
216. (a)	217. (b)	218. (d)	219. (a)	220. (d)
221. (a)	222. (b)	223. (c)	224. (b)	225. (c)
226. (a)	227. (d)	228. (b)	229. (c)	230. (b)
231. (d)	232. (d)	233. (b)	234. (a)	235. (b)
236. (d)	237. (b)	238. (a)	239. (b)	240. (a)
241. (d)	242. (b)	243. (c)	244. (b)	245. (a)
246. (b)	247. (a)	248. (c)	249. (c)	250. (a)
251. (b)	252. (a)	253. (d)	254. (b)	255. (d)
256. (a)	257. (b)	258. (b)	259. (b)	260. (c)
261. (b)	262. (c)	263. (d)	264. (d)	265. (d)
266. (b)	267. (c)	268. (a)	269. (b)	270. (a)
271. (a)	272. (b)	273. (a)	274. (b)	275. (c)
276. (b)	277. (a)	278. (b)	279. (a)	280. (b)
281. (a)	282. (b)	283. (d)	284. (b)	285. (c)

286. (b)	287. (a)	288. (c)	289. (b)	290. (a)
291. (a)	292. (b)	293. (b)	294. (a)	295. (c)
296. (a)	297. (c)	298. (b)	299. (d)	300. (b)
301. (c)	302. (b)	303. (c)	304. (d)	305. (a)
306. (b)	307. (c)	308. (a)	309. (b)	310. (d)
311. (a)	312. (a)	313. (d)	314. (b)	315. (a)
316. (c)	317. (b)	318. (d)	319. (a)	320. (b)
321. (c)	322. (a)	323. (a)	324. (b)	325. (b)
326. (a)	327. (c)	328. (a)	329. (c)	330. (c)
331. (a)	332. (d)	333. (d)	334. (b)	335. (a)
336. (b)	337. (a)	338. (b)	339. (c)	340. (a)
341. (b)	342. (c)	343. (a)	344. (a)	345. (a)
346. (b)	347. (c)	348. (d)	349. (c)	350. (b)
351. (a)	352. (b)	353. (b)	354. (c)	355. (b)
356. (a)	357. (a)	358. (c)	359. (b)	360. (b)
361. (a)	362. (a)	363. (d)	364. (c)	365. (b)
366. (d)	367. (b)	368. (a)	369. (d)	370. (d)
371. (c)	372. (c)	373. (a)	374. (b)	375. (a)
376. (a)	377. (b)	378. (b)	379. (a)	380. (c)
381. (d)	382. (a)	383. (d)	384. (b)	385. (b)
386. (c)	387. (a)	388. (b)	389. (c)	390. (a)
391. (b)	392. (d)	393. (a)	394. (b)	395. (b)
396. (c)	397. (a)	398. (b)	399. (d)	400. (b)
401. (c)	402. (a)	403. (d)	404. (b)	405. (c)
406. (a)	407. (b)	408. (b)	409. (b)	410. (c)
411. (b)	412. (a)	413. (c)	414. (a)	415. (b)
416. (c)	417. (a)	418. (b)	419. (a)	420. (b)
421. (a)	422. (d)	423. (a)	424. (c)	425. (b)
426. (c)	427. (a)	428. (b)	429. (c)	430. (b)

431. (c)	432. (b)	433. (c)	434. (a)	435. (b)
436. (c)	437. (d)	438. (a)	439. (a)	440. (d)
441. (b)	442. (d)	443. (a)	444. (b)	445. (a)
446. (d)	447. (b)	448. (c)	449. (b)	450. (a)
451. (a)	452. (b)	453. (c)	454. (d)	455. (b)
456. (a)	457. (c)	458. (a)	459. (a)	460. (b)
461. (c)	462. (a)	463. (b)	464. (a)	465. (d)
466. (b)	467. (c)	468. (a)	469. (b)	470. (b)
471. (c)	472. (d)	473. (a)	474. (b)	475. (b)
476. (c)	477. (a)	478. (a)	479. (c)	480. (b)
481. (b)	482. (a)	483. (d)	484. (b)	485. (a)
486. (b)	487. (d)	488. (b)	489. (c)	490. (a)
491. (b)	492. (a)	493. (c)	494. (b)	495. (a)
496. (b)	497. (a)	498. (b)	499. (d)	500. (a)
501. (d)	502. (d)	503. (a)	504. (c)	505. (d)
506. (a)	507. (b)	508. (a)	509. (c)	510. (b)
511. (b)	512. (a)	513. (b)	514. (a)	515. (c)
516. (b)	517. (b)	518. (d)	519. (b)	520. (d)
521. (a)	522. (d)	523. (c)	524. (a)	525. (a)
526. (c)	527. (a)	528. (c)	529. (c)	530. (d)
531. (c)	532. (b)	533. (c)	534. (b)	535. (b)
536. (a)	537. (b)	538. (b)	539. (b)	540. (d)
541. (b)	542. (a)	543. (c)	544. (a)	545. (b)
546. (d)	547. (b)	548. (d)	549. (a)	550. (b)
551. (b)	552. (a)	553. (d)	554. (d)	555. (c)
556. (d)	557. (b)	558. (c)	559. (b)	560. (a)
561. (b)	562. (a)	563. (b)	564. (b)	565. (d)
566. (c)	567. (d)	568. (b)	569. (a)	570. (d)
571. (b)	572. (c)	573. (b)	574. (c)	575. (b)

576.(c)	577.(d)	578.(b)	579.(d)	580.(a)
581.(b)	582.(d)	583.(a)	584.(c)	585.(b)
586.(a)	587.(d)	588.(b)	589.(b)	590.(d)
591.(b)	592.(b)	593.(a)	594.(c)	595.(b)
596.(d)	597.(c)	598.(a)	599.(b)	600.(a)
601.(c)	602.(b)	603.(d)	604.(a)	605.(b)
606.(a)	607.(b)	608.(a)	609.(b)	610.(c)
611.(c)	612.(d)	613.(a)	614.(b)	615.(d)
616.(a)	617.(d)	618.(b)	619.(b)	620.(c)
621.(a)	622.(c)	623.(a)	624.(b)	625.(a)
626.(c)	627.(d)	628.(c)	629.(c)	630.(d)
631.(d)	632.(d)	633.(b)	634.(d)	635.(c)
636.(d)	637.(d)	638.(a)	639.(b)	640.(c)
641.(c)	642.(a)	643.(b)	644.(c)	645.(c)
646.(b)	647.(d)	648.(c)	649.(a)	650.(c)
651.(b)	652.(a)	653.(a)	654.(b)	655.(a)
656.(d)	657.(b)	658.(b)	659.(b)	660.(d)
661.(a)	662.(b)	663.(c)	664.(d)	665.(b)
666.(a)	667.(a)	668.(d)	669.(c)	670.(a)
671.(d)	672.(c)	673.(a)	674.(a)	675.(b)
676.(b)	677.(b)	678.(a)	679.(d)	680.(b)
681.(c)	682.(b)	683.(d)	684.(a)	685.(c)
686.(a)	687.(c)	688.(b)	689.(b)	690.(a)
691.(b)	692.(a)	693.(d)	694.(c)	695.(b)
696.(c)	697.(a)	698.(b)	699.(c)	700.(a)
701.(b)	702.(a)	703.(d)	704.(b)	705.(d)
706.(a)	707.(c)	708.(b)	709.(c)	710.(b)
711.(d)	712.(a)	713.(d)	714.(d)	715.(a)
716.(b)	717.(b)	718.(a)	719.(b)	720.(c)

721. (a)	722. (d)	723. (a)	724. (c)	725. (b)
726. (c)	727. (c)	728. (d)	729. (b)	730. (b)
731. (a)	732. (b)	733. (c)	734. (a)	735. (d)
736. (c)	737. (d)	738. (b)	739. (a)	740. (c)
741. (a)	742. (a)	743. (a)	744. (b)	745. (c)
746. (d)	747. (b)	748. (b)	749. (a)	750. (b)
751. (a)	752. (d)	753. (c)	754. (a)	755. (b)
756. (b)	757. (c)	758. (b)	759. (a)	760. (b)
761. (c)	762. (d)	763. (c)	764. (d)	765. (a)
766. (b)	767. (b)	768. (b)	769. (a)	770. (c)
771. (b)	772. (a)	773. (b)	774. (c)	775. (a)
776. (c)	777. (b)	778. (d)	779. (c)	780. (c)
781. (c)	782. (b)	783. (a)	784. (b)	785. (b)
786. (c)	787. (a)	788. (c)	789. (b)	790. (a)
791. (b)	792. (c)	793. (a)	794. (b)	795. (a)
796. (d)	797. (c)	798. (d)	799. (b)	800. (d)
801. (a)	802. (c)	803. (d)	804. (d)	805. (a)
806. (b)	807. (d)	808. (b)	809. (d)	810. (d)
811. (c)	812. (d)	813. (d)	814. (b)	815. (a)
816. (d)	817. (a)	818. (b)	819. (c)	820. (b)
821. (a)	822. (b)	823. (c)	824. (b)	825. (c)
826. (b)	827. (d)	828. (b)	829. (b)	830. (c)
831. (a)	832. (b)	833. (c)	834. (d)	835. (c)
836. (d)	837. (a)	838. (b)	839. (a)	840. (b)
841. (b)	842. (a)	843. (d)	844. (a)	845. (b)
846. (c)	847. (d)	848. (b)	849. (a)	850. (c)
851. (d)	852. (c)	853. (a)	854. (a)	855. (a)
856. (d)	857. (c)	858. (a)	859. (b)	860. (c)
861. (a)	862. (b)	863. (c)	864. (a)	865. (d)

866. (b)	867. (a)	868. (a)	869. (a)	870. (b)
871. (d)	872. (b)	873. (a)	874. (d)	875. (d)
876. (b)	877. (d)	878. (b)	879. (d)	880. (a)
881. (b)	882. (d)	883. (b)	884. (c)	885. (b)
886. (a)	887. (c)	888. (a)	889. (b)	890. (d)
891. (a)	892. (b)	893. (d)	894. (d)	895. (d)
896. (d)	897. (a)	898. (b)	839. (a)	900. (b)
901. (b)	902. (a)	903. (c)	904. (a)	905. (c)
906. (a)	907. (a)	908. (b)	909. (a)	910. (b)
911. (a)	912. (c)	913. (b)	914. (d)	915. (c)
916. (b)	917. (b)	918. (a)	919. (d)	920. (d)
921. (a)	922. (c)	923. (c)	924. (a)	925. (b)
926. (a)	927. (d)	928. (c)	929. (b)	930. (c)
931. (b)	932. (c)	933. (a)	934. (b)	935. (c)
936. (a)	937. (b)	938. (d)	939. (a)	940. (b)
941. (d)	942. (a)	943. (b)	944. (a)	945. (d)
946. (b)	947. (a)	948. (d)	949. (b)	950. (c)
951. (a)	952. (b)	953. (d)	954. (b)	955. (b)
956. (c)	957. (d)	958. (b)	959. (a)	960. (d)
961. (d)	962. (d)	963. (b)	964. (a)	965. (c)
966. (c)	967. (b)	968. (c)	969. (a)	970. (c)
971. (b)	972. (b)	973. (b)	974. (d)	975. (d)

976. Vitamin C
977. Diazepam
978. Aspirin
979. Paracetamol
980. Tuberculosis
981. B Group
982. Dapsone
983. Chloramphenicol
984. Vitamin B6
985. Antibiotic
986. Antibacterial
987. Hodgkin's disease

988. Chloro-
quine

989. Meben-
dazole

990. Benzocaine

991. Thyroxine

992. Antibiotic

993. Vitamin B$_1$

994. Analgin

995. Mercuro-
chrome

996. Griseo-
fulvin

997. Scabies

998. Otoscope

999. Cerebrum

1000. (a) Incisors (b) Canine (c) Premolars